FORTRESS WALES

Jonathan Powell

Trafford rev. 06/29/2017

 www.trafford.com
North America & international
toll-free: 1 888 232 4444 (USA & Canada)
fax: 812 355 4082

Front Cover: White Castle. (Image - The Photolibrary Wales)

AUTHOR'S NOTE

This book would of not been possible without first and foremost the blessing of 'Country Quest', who published many of my castle articles over a period of nearly three years, so my thanks to them and especially its editor.

I would also like to thank Steve Benbow at The Photolibrary Wales for his time and assistance.

The book is dedicated to all those who simply love castles, not solely because of their complex history, but because they look amazing to the eye, and never fail to to leave me in awe of their grandness.

INTRODUCTION

Wales has more castles per square mile of landscape, then anywhere else in Europe, meaning that across the country, you are never really far away from one of these historic sites.

For me, castles are a truly fascinating representation of bygone years, a standing testimony to the times of Wales' turbulent past. A striking reminder of a fight for independence, when different nations saw much to be taken from the Welsh homeland.

The name of Owain Glyndwr is synonymous with the struggle to keep Wales for the Welsh. A true champion of the fight against the aggressor, (in this case the English), Glyndwr is a man who took his feuding beyond just a war of words, turning it into a violent nationwide rebellion against those who had made the Welsh slaves on their own turf. Turning the tide against the trespassers who had invaded Wales and imposed land rent and regulated tenancies, and many other degrading laws against its acquired citizens.

In 1399, Glyndwr, a prominent landowner at the time, had had enough of this oppression, and turned his bitter feud with Lord Grey of Ruthin, into an all out uprising across the nation, and in doing so, earned himself the title of Prince of Wales.

His strategy to drive the English out centred not upon battlefield showdowns, but on using the Welsh terrain to cause havoc, with surprise attacks and calculated ambushes, in an attempt to gradually weaken the invader. The castles that had been built by these unwelcome rulers though, were eventually to prove too much for Glyndwr, and despite many successful raids on these strongholds, and many victories to his name, the castles that had been built to keep peace over the Welsh, finally achieved their aim, and the revolt was crushed.

For his absolute conviction and determination, Owain Glyndwr embodied all of the Welsh struggle, with his dedicated army even acquiring the name 'Owain's Children'.

Although, all was not in vain, it was a reminder of what the Welsh were capable of, and also that castles were in fact vulnerable, and once a castle wall is breached, its legendary 'unbreachable' boast is gone forever.

When you see a castle for the first time, I often try to envisage it at the height of its splendour, with a resident garrison, surrounding village folk going about their every day business, and the accompanying smells and atmosphere of the time. In doing so, one obtains a real sense of what a castle is all about, not just a hard faced stone military stronghold, but a focal point for a community that has settled within its walls and surrounding it, a beacon if you will to all that approach it, and a symbol of strength and unity for all around to see.

Whilst there is an absolute wealth to be learned from each castle, which has its own unique story to tell, for me, just seeing one of these majestic fortresses is enough to fire-up a passion about history, accompanied by a great feeling of awe.

There's this castle, standing before you, a centuries old piece of architecture, in some cases virtually unscathed, and whether it be near modern buildings or set within the beautiful Welsh countryside, it cannot fail to impress and give the onlooker a sense that this is touchable, hands-on innovation of its time, a monument to the past that anyone can enjoy and admire.

So, upon visiting any site, adjust your gaze away from the pages of this book, stand back, and take in the castle before you, because as plain as day and away from any lecture theatre or classroom, there stands history.

CHRONICLE OF EARLY
WELSH MILITARY HISTORY

AD 49 Romans invade South Wales.

410 Roman rule ends in Britain.

490 Saxons are beaten by Arthur.

851 Commencement of Danish attacks on Britain.

1067 Norman influence of Wales begins as they enter South Wales. Marcher Lords over the coming years establish themselves on the Welsh borders. In 1087, William II succeeds William the Conqueror.

1100 Henry I becomes king.

1135 With Norman influence spreading across Wales, Henry I dies and England is thrown into turbulent civil war. Owain Gwynedd drives the Norman forces out of North Wales.

1154 Henry II becomes king. Rhys ap Gruffydd dominates South Wales as he rises to power.

1165 Welsh defeat Henry's army

1175 Other territories regained by the Welsh.

1188 Traveller, historian and ecclesiastic Gerald of Wales writes his 'Itinerary'.

1189 Richard I, (Lionheart), is crowned king. Llywelyn ap Iorwerth becomes prominent for the Welsh.

1199 John becomes king.

1215 Magna Carta installs new Welsh rights. Territories also returned to the Welsh.

1216 Henry III becomes king.

1258 Llywelyn ap Gruffydd claims power in Wales, later to be recognised by Henry III.

1272 Edward I becomes king.

1277 With bitterness between Llywelyn and Edward, starting with Llywelyn's refusal to attend Edward's coronation, Edward now invades Wales following border attacks by the Welsh. In the following years the Treaty of Rhuddlan is signed as Llywelyn sues for peace. Edwardian castles erected to maintain peace.

1282 Edward attacks again as Welsh combination of Llywelyn and Dafydd provoke war. Welsh crumble and weakened in defeat. More Edwardian castles erected in coming years.

1307 Edward II becomes king.

1327 Edward III becomes king.

1377 Richard II becomes king.

1399 Henry IV becomes king.

1400 Owain Glyndwr leads his first uprising.

1410 Despite French support and many victories, the rebellion crumbles and Owain Glyndwr disappears.

1413 Henry V becomes king.

1415 French defeated at Agincourt.

1422 Henry VI becomes king.

1455 War of the Roses begins.

1461 Edward VI becomes king.

1483 Richard III becomes king.

1485   Richard III killed at Bosworth, Henry VII becomes king.

1509   Henry VIII becomes king.

1547   Edward VI becomes king.

1553   Mary I becomes queen.

1558   Elizabeth I becomes queen.

1603   James I becomes king.

1625   Charles I becomes king.

1642 to 1651

> The Welsh throw their weight behind the Royalist cause in Wales during the Civil War. Charles I is later executed and as Charles II flees English turf, Cromwell sets about slighting castles. In doing so, the once mighty castle now begins a fall from grace, with its time of dominance now becoming resigned to history.

HISTORY OF CASTLES
IN WALES

The earliest defensive structures on Welsh soil date back to around 1,000 BC, the late Bronze Age, and were mainly of simple construction, in the form of a hillfort.

The Romans built many of their forts on territory that they had conquered in the years following AD 43, and as many other invaders were to find, Wales and the Marches proved especially difficult for them to seize, taking them nearly a quarter of a century to add to their empire. Total victory over the the Welsh wasn't to be for mighty Rome however, thanks to Boudicca's rebellion in AD 60 which generally put all matters on hold for the Romans in this part of the world.

In later years, following on from initial fortresses at Usk and Wroexter, and then much later at Caerleon and Chester, 36 auxiliary forts were built with the aim of finally quashing and silencing the Welsh. With this, peace, albeit uneasy until Rome's occupation showed benefits, ensued.

It was the Normans however, who introduced the castle as we know it into Wales, starting on the Welsh Marches and gradually pushing into the heartland over a period of years.

William the Conqueror initially entrusted the borders of Wales to three prominent noblemen of the time. William FitzOsbern, Earl of Hereford, was given the south of the Marches to oversee, with the central part in the hands of Roger Montgomery, Earl of Shrewsbury, and the north to Hugh of Avranches, Earl of Chester.

Although the building of castles was mainly considered to be a case of keeping the Welsh in their own territory, it wasn't long before all three noblemen decided to make inroads into Wales of their own accord.

The first castles to be erected were of a simple motte and bailey design, comprising a simple timber construction on top of a mound, which may or may not, have included buildings inside. As the Welsh though resisted later on, it became necessary to make these fortifications more durable against attack, and so stone was now used as standard.

Whilst there was stiff opposition in the north to the progress made by the Earl of Chester, the rest of Wales succumbed to Norman force, with Montgomery making remarkable progress right across Powys and on into Dyfed, claiming it for himself, and appointing one of his sons as lord. The son, Anulf, was to build Pembroke Castle, which over time with much rebuilding, became a mighty fortress.

From 1131, the Clare family, prominent in Chepstow and using the castle as their base, founded Tintern Abbey and went to build no fewer than nine castles, including Aberystwyth.

The next generation of the Clare family even had their eyes on Ireland and grew so much in stature, that they became the most powerful Marcher family of the 13th century, with Caerphilly Castle being testimony to their accumulated wealth and status.

The three initial 'Marcher lordships' and the subsequent history that entailed, from the various conquests that future generations were to make across Wales, was to last for centuries, until the Acts of Union with England in 1536-42.

The Normans during this time not only used their strategic influence to capture Wales, but also made great use of the substantial discord within Welsh families, where bitter rivalry within the family over land, would cause internal ructions, which meant there was already an inharmonious situation in existence, one to be capitalised upon and used to the Normans advantage.

Despite the advances across Welsh territory by the 'Marcher lordships' there was resistance, mainly due to the Welsh often adapting and using the tactics that had initially driven them back. Two such power bases were constructed and held by Owain Gwynedd in the north west of Wales, and Rhys ap Gruffydd, more commonly known as Lords Rhys, in Deheubarth.

These two gradually built their own castles and together with castles wrestled from the Normans, expanded their own empire's across the land, reclaiming fallen territory as they did so. Strangely enough, Rhys and Owain would think nothing of attacking other Welsh rulers, with even more oddly, sometimes incorporating an alliance with the Normans in order to do so.

Llywelyn ap Iorwerth was to next build up his power in the north, with his own empire expanding in Gwynedd, as he became known as Llywelyn the Great.

Upon Llewelyn's death, the Welsh and Normans fought for what he had created, until Llewelyn's grandson vowed to get back what his grandfather had built. The grandson, Llywelyn ap Gruffydd, was to be known as our last leader, as Edward I swept all before him, including this disputed land.

Edward I was to build many an impressive fortress, in an attempt to stamp his authority across north and mid Wales, and it wasn't until Owain Glyndwr's revolt, that peace was shattered in the 1400's.

Much later, when another chapter in history closed as the War of the Roses ended in 1485, (following 30 years of unrest), a lot was to change when Henry VII was crowned king. The Tudor dynasty meant a shift from turmoil to more peaceful times in Wales.

Castles were beginning to be abandoned in favour of manor houses, but despite this trend, it was not the end of their use.

When Civil War broke out 1642, then again with a second war in 1648, many castles were soon back in military use, and it is upon the ending of these two particular conflicts, that the castle really did meet its downfall.

Many castles were slighted when the Civil War ended, damaged beyond use as military bases, some were literally dismantled and the stone used elsewhere, others damaged to the state of total ruin. Thus, castles became no longer viable for military use, or for use as living accommodation.

Despite attempts to restore many of them to their former glory over the coming centuries, this really did signal the end of the era in which these mighty stone giants ruled the countryside.

No longer would castles fulfil the purpose for which they were built, but as with many things in life, this was natural progression, sad though it was at the time.

That said, there are quite a few castles not in a ruinous state, carefully looked after and preserved as treasured buildings, so really, although they may not be the dominant force that they were, the tale of the castle is alive and well, and on view for all to see.

LAYOUT OF A CASTLE

For the purpose of this text, we shall assume the 'blueprint' type of castle that we can all relate too. A typical concentric castle, built on a mound with the usual defences and features associated with a castle of this nature. This will also be the image many of us first conjure up in our minds when we think of a fortress, that too, is the power of their imagery within current thought.

As the attacker advances towards the castle from the front, there may well be a counterscarp directly ahead of them. This is a rise in the ground in front of them on approach, varying in height, but never the less, a purpose built rise. In warfare, military strategy has always dictated that it is easier to fight a battle going downhill than uphill, hence the counterscarp, even though it may not be on 'Hollywood' style grandeur.

Having reached the top of the rise, the approaching army would be faced by a deep moat or in lesser cases, a wet ditch, as with all defences situated outside the castle, proclaiming to be just one more obstacle to hold them up, and to give the garrison residing inside the fortification, a chance to barrage the aggressor with anything they can lay their hands on, from arrows to rocks.

At this point, of course, the attacker would have had aerial support as they motioned forwards towards the castle, probably in the form of a ballista. This was an early mis-sile propelling weapon, resembling a large crossbow on a portable carriage. From it, greeting the barrage from within the castle, they would return fire with arrows, stones and most effectively, metal bolts.

Another effective weapon was also the mangonel, a siege engine used for hurling particularly heavy stones.

Once the moat was forged, there is generally another scarp to ascend which leads up to the outer curtain wall, a ring of wall which goes right around the perimeter of the castle, acting as a first solid line of defence.

There may well be small open backed towers at intervals around this outer curtain, allowing the occupants to further impede the attacking force by discharging other weaponry from these protruding parts of the wall.

Over this curtain wall will bring the attacker into the outer bailey, otherwise known as a courtyard or ward of the castle, which will also be heavily defended.

Attached to the castle and enveloping a section of the outer bailey may well be the barbican, which is fortified outwork built to defend the gatehouse which it would of enclosed. There would be guards ready to defend both the barbican, outer bailey and castle entrance itself.

Upon breaching the barbican, the attacker would attempt to either climb the wall of the castle proper, (the castle walls being set back from the defensive ring of the outer curtain), or storm the gatehouse directly, the gatehouse being the main entrance to the castle.

You can probably also see by now, that attacking a fortress without sufficient numbers would make the task virtually impossible, with the design of the castle built soley with defence in mind.

The gatehouse will be well defended too, with a portcullis protecting the entrance, raised and lowered by winches within the gatehouse itself.

Should the attacker manage to breach this, they may find themselves covered in all manner of things, from oil to rocks, as special openings in the upper part of the gatehouse, 'murderholes', were used, down which guards could pour whatever they had to hand onto the unsuspecting and unwanted visitors below.

'Murderholes' were situated in the roofs and passageways, especially entrances, through which attackers could be ambushed, either by pouring substances on them, or by guards physically using them to drop onto the ground below, using the element of surprise.

Should anybody wishing to seize the castle decide to scale the actual castle walls, rather than attack the gatehouse directly, they would probably have used a siege tower, or 'belfry'. These were wooden towers mounted on wheels, often covered with wet hide to prevent them being burned from flaming arrows fired at it.

These wooden towers would be wheeled or rolled up, (if on rollers), to the wall, and via drop-bridges at the top of the tower, give access to the wall walks situated on the inside of castle wall, or even the towers situated at intervening points along the inner curtain.

They could also have used a 'bore', an iron-tipped battering ram type weapon, used for attacking masonry, this would hopefully smash directly through the wall, by punching its way through, rather than having to have gone over the top with a siege tower.

The battlements situated at the top of the inner curtain wall also provided defence for the castle occupants. They protrude somewhat out of the wall, and in the bottom of this jutting piece of the battlements, more holes had been designed, so like the 'murderholes', these machicolations as they are known, would allow the defenders to shoot missiles vertically on the attackers below, or indeed, pour something on them.

Looking like a bottom set of teeth on a jaw are the merlon, the 'teeth' of the battlements, with the lower parts between them being referred to as crenal or embrasure.

The 'teeth' also had a slight inclination to them, this is called the chamfer.

Finally on the underside of the battlements is the corbel, a piece of projecting stone or timber on the inner curtain, used to support the battlements themselves, but also used as a general support to anything along the curtain, from the parapets, (a protective wall on the outer side of a wall walk), to the turrets.

Castles of this design would more than likely have had a smaller gatehouse situated at the rear of the castle, generally no with barbican, but none the less well defended, offering the occupants a back door to the castle so to speak.

There would also of been a postern, which is a small gate or door, situated usually some distance from the entrance to the castle, again at the rear. These well hidden 'sallyports', allowed the home garrison to slip out of the castle unnoticed to either execute a sharp exit were things not going to plan, or as a military manoeuvre, to carry out a flank attack on the besiegers.

Within the castle itself, the solar was the name given to the private living quarters of the lord, usually situated not far from the great hall.

With the great hall and solar finally seized, all would now be considered lost, and as with so many castles throughout the years, a new owner would now preside.

It's surprising how many castles were actually taken by the invader, taken back again, and then retaken. Of course many attempts to seize castles failed, but there were few castles that escaped some sort of involvement across Wales, many though, were to see more than their fair share.

ABERGAVENNY CASTLE

Travel down on the A465 from Hereford and you enter Wales via the 'Gateway' town of Abergavenny. Travel deep into the town until you near the river Usk and you'll find its castle. Built in the 12th Century, it was a stage for scenes of treachery, revenge and bitter power struggles involving the Normans, the English and the Welsh.

The name of William de Braose, a Norman lord, is synonymous with the horrific events that took place at the castle, earning him the reputation of being one of cruellest and most wicked men of the 12th Century period.

In the late 12th Century, one of the most notable Welsh leaders in Gwent, was Seisyll ap Dyfnwal.

In 1175 Seisyll killed Henry who had been Lord of Breconshire, this title including Abergavenny in its realm. Henry, son of the Earl of Hereford, had a brother named Mahel, but when he too died after being struck by a falling stone during a fire at Bronllys castle, (a small knight's castle some seven miles away), the Lordship was succeeded by William de Braose, nephew to the Earl.

In 1176 de Braose set about planning revenge for what had taken place by inviting Seisyll to what was called 'a peace conference' and a celebration of Christmas at Abergavenny castle. Seisyll and his son Geoffrey, the most renowned and powerful chieftains of Powys, were amongst many other Welsh captains who had been invited from the surrounding area to attend what had seemed to be on the face of it, nothing more than a 'local summit'. So taken in by the offer were the chiefs, that they came unarmed into what turned out to be a blood bath, where the Welshmen were slaughtered one by one, as de Braose committed ultimate revenge for the death of his uncle.

William de Braose then turned his attention to Seisyll's own fortress, Castell Arnallt, destroying it and murdering Seisyll's wife and other son Cadwaladr.

He also set about killing other chieftains, and their wives and children, in a relentless quest to make the revenge a far reaching and far damaging one within the Welsh community.

In carrying out this act at the castle, de Braose had broken one of the most highly regarded ideals of the Welsh code, where the concept of hospitality to one's guest, was deemed to be a very important and honoured practice.

From that day on, the surviving sons of the murdered Welsh chieftains vowed revenge with their fellow men for this atrocity.

Several attempts were made to instigate such revenge. On one such occasion, the Welshmen tried to enter Abergavenny castle by night over the battlements. A later attempt did however succeed as the Welsh scaled the walls of castle with ladders, eventually capturing the castle with its governor, wife and entire garrison. With reference to the event, Anglo-Welsh Churchman and chronicler of Welsh life during these times, Gerald of Wales wrote that 'God in his justice thus decreed that the original crime should be punished on the very spot where it had been committed'.

Years later this very act of capturing the castle was repeated again, this time by William, son of the Earl of Hereford.

Like William de Braose's revenge, the Welsh made their own revenge felt widely, as they turned their attention to Ranulf Poer, Sheriff of Herefordshire who had actually carried out the murders during the 'peace conference'.

As Poer, a close crony of de Braose's, and his men were in the process of building a castle near Dingestow, Monmouth, the Welsh stormed it and along with nine leading Norman captains of Gwent, killed him. William de Braose was also present at Dingestow during its construction and had to rely on the bravery of his own men to save him, having fallen into a deep trench.

Following his timely rescue, de Braose escaped to pursue his conquests only until King John, once a close ally of his, turned against him, leaving him destitute in exile, whilst his wife and eldest child were left to die of starvation at Windsor Castle.

It is interesting to note, that during the siege at Abergavenny castle, a piece of the history that went into making the bow men of the Welsh armies so feared occurred. For it is in 1182, that a four inch thick oak door was pierced right through by Welsh arrows. Such

a monumental and awesome sight it was, to see iron tips on the inside of doors, that the tips became display pieces to passers-by and visitors, a true spectacle of the might of the Welsh bowmen and their archery skills.

As time passed the English kings were forced to recruit such bowmen from Wales into their own armies, as they were deemed unbeatable. It is recounted that during the campaigns of Edward I, there were bowmen in his army from Gwent and Crickhowell.

In 1215, Llewellyn ap Iorweth, (The Great), captured Abergavenny Castle from the forces of King John, during the baronial revolt against John, who had seen Llewellyn as far to powerful for his own good, even if Llewellyn was his son-in-law.

Many years later, Llewellyn was to form alliances with English barons against King John, who had lost much support in his kingdom, and their interests to safeguard the personal claims and interests of the Welsh people, are documented in three clauses of the Magna Carta.

Abergavenny castle avoided complete destruction in 1403, during the revolt of Owain Glyndwr, as the town was burnt during the uprising in which Glyndwr had tried to reaffirm Welsh identity amidst English suppression. Although the revolt itself apparently failed, with new laws forbidding Welshmen to acquire land within the limits of border towns being implicated, it had certainly instilled national awareness in Wales of the injustice on their land.

Until the Civil War, the castle enjoyed relative peace, with the Barony of Abergavenny being conferred on the possessor of the castle.

During the Civil War in 1645, Parliamentarian forces caused great damage to the castle and with the passing of time, the castle now stands as a ruin. The "most goodly towers" as the poet Churchyard proclaimed them, (two square towers), and a gate with a substantial barbican, are all that is left remaining, accompanied by an adjacent modern mansion.

A museum now resides in the grounds of castle, both of which are open to the public.

The castle is situated at the south end of the town. Head for Abergavenny using either the A465 if coming from Merthyr Tydfil, or if approaching from Monmouth or Raglan, use the A40.s

B

BEAUPRE CASTLE

Beaupre Castle can be reached by footpath, some 2 miles outside of Cowbridge. Pronounced 'bewper', this lonely stronghold is set amidst pleasant green fields and was home to the Bassets, descended from the earliest Norman settlers and whose family motto declared 'Better death than shame'.

To get to Beaupre, first find Cowbridge itself, which is situated in the Vale of Glamorgan and held in many people's opinion as the Capital of the Vale. From there, walk south-east from the town to just outside a place called St. Hilary, and there stands the castle. You will see that the literal translation of the old French "beau-repaire" states a 'Beautiful Retreat', which this castle certainly merits.

This CADW cared for site, is one of the two main attractions in this part of the world, the other being Llanerch Vineyard at Hensol, Pendoyslan. It's worth mentioning because this vineyard produces Wales's only commercially estate-bottled wine, and upon visiting, there is wine tasting to be had!

There is another castle situated in the area, Old Castle, at Llanblethian near Cowbridge. Research has revealed not as much as the better documented Beaupre Castle, but it appears that some historians during Tudor times made references to it, calling it Llygod Castle. Curiously enough, the castle is shown in the background of a popular 18th Century painting, but apart from this, no details are known about it or about its supposed predecessor, Llanblethian Castle.

In stark contrast, the history at Beaupre Castle charts the domination of it by the Basset family, who were responsible for the earliest construction on its present day site during the 13th Century, remaining in their family name until 1709.

The castle, also known as 'Old Beaupre' (because of an construction in the 19th Century of a 'New Beaupre' mansion) consisted firstly of a group of buildings, built inside the inner of two courtyards.

Situated on a steep bank in a curve of the River Thaw, the Castle, although built with some defensive purpose in mind, was always a peaceful residence, which calls into question its status as a Castle. Untouched by the forces of Owain Glyndwr, it has seen no battles or any such military involvement over its long years. Granted, you don't have to be involved in a long a bloody siege to gain Castle status, but some may argue it is a manor house and nothing more.

Having researched its defences however, I am inclined to agree that its Castle status is rightful, let alone the fact that it simply does look like a Castle anyway.

First of all its siting. Built next to the River Thaw for observation of any crossings and incorporating a steep bank, making access up to the Castle from this approach difficult.

Secondly, the 18 feet high medieval curtain wall once boasted castellations or battlements and thirdly, there are to this day, the remains of a substantial gatehouse.

All classic pointers towards a defensible position, a stronghold, and in my opinion, more than just a simple manor house.

By the 16th Century, the medieval buildings were all but abandoned and what we see of the castle today, is where history picks up following a great rebuilding program at the castle.

The program was started by Sir Rice Mansel

and concluded many years later by the then Sir Richard Basset.

Sir Rice is responsible for the earliest part of the Tudor additions, in around 1540. Amongst his work is a three storey building, now unfortunately roofless and floorless. In its time, this would of been of classic Tudor design and decor, boasting the very best of luxurious living accommodation with large windows, fireplaces and stairways.

In his redevelopment of the site as an Elizabethan mansion, Sir Richard was to add the most important feature at Beaupre Castle, the outer gatehouse and storeyed porch, probably the finest of its kind in Wales.

These are remarkably well preserved from this era, with only the gatehouse and adjacent curtain wall surviving from the medieval stage.

Its lavish blend of Elizabethan and Jacobean times, and the undoubted wealth of the Basset family, make this an extravagant piece of workmanship. The heraldic panels and inscriptions leave you in no doubt as to its maker. Richly carved and carrying Sir Richard's Coat of Arms on a central shield above the doorway, it is truly a work of art.

The porch was built to a very high standard with the majority of its details surviving the ravages of time. With its Tudor archway and classical columns, the porch is also incorporates in its building, the earliest known use of brick in Glamorgan, situated in the porch's inner facing.

As with any great piece of architecture, Sir

Richard has left his own inscription, stating that he built this porch in 1600.

And what of the man Sir Richard himself?. He was a faithful loyalist, appointed High Sheriff in 1645 and made governor of Cardiff Castle in 1645 by Charles I. Unfortunately, Sir Richard found himself to be unpopular in his position at Cardiff, and decided to surrender his commission to the King.

His misfortune continued when on his way to surrender the commission in Hereford, he was captured by the rival Parliamentarian forces, as the city had fallen shortly before from Royalist hands and into their enemy's control. This piece of bad luck cost him £753 in fines.

The decline at Beaupre Castle seems to stem from these series of events, which ultimately led to the Castle's eventual abandonment. Sir Richard's son took ownership next, making enough of an impact in his world to merit a burial at Westminster Abbey.

The last to own the Castle in the Basset bloodline was the eldest son of William's half-brother, eventually falling out of the family's name, passing into many other hands before becoming the care of the Department of the Environment, with very few alterations made to it since the redevelopment work of Sir Richard.

There is an adjacent private farmhouse and buildings, located to the south of Beaupre which once served as an inner court, and only here is there some evidence of some early 18th Century panelling, these I hasten to add, not open to the public.

Beaupre Castle is however open to the public with free entrance, although there are access restrictions to some parts.

BRECON CASTLE

With its charming narrow streets and promenade overlooking the River Usk, Brecon remains a town virtually untouched by the hand of the modern developer. Unfortunately, where the road builders have been is Brecon Castle, slicing her in two to produce Norman architecture with a strip of tarmac through the middle.

Away from the town centre on a hill top stands the castle. With striking views of the Brecon Beacons, the one half of the castle to the south is integrated into Brecon Castle Hotel. Across the road are the remains of the 12th century Ely Tower, so-called after the imprisonment of John Morton, Bishop of Ely within its walls - all of which are in the garden of the current Bishop of Swansea and Brecon.

The history in and around the site of the castle dates back some 4000 to 5000 years, with evidence of the manufacture of flint tools discoverd here. There are also the remains of Pen-y-crug, an Iron Age Hill Fort.

Two miles west of Brecon is Y Gaer Roman Fort. This was an important Roman stronghold with its construction dated around 50 A.D. The fort covers an area of some 5 acres and it is thought that the first regiment to occupy it were from North West Spain.

Brecon, which derives its name from

'Brychan', the son of an Irish Prince, had its first fortress built here at the end of the 11th Century, on the site of where the castle stands today.

It's creator was Bernard de Newmarch, a relative of William the Conqueror, and the early construction took the form of a simple motte and bailey. There was originally a timber keep and the courtyard below the motte extended to cover the garden, now owned by the bishop.

Newmarch had captured the kingdom of Brycheiniog from the Welsh rulers in 1093, and set about building castles to protect and oversee his newly gained land beneath the Beacons, which boast the highest peaks in South Wales.

On obtaining the lands from the princes, Newmarch was made Lord of Brecon and granted numerous rights. He could also see the value of the position he now commanded, meaning that the castle would have to be strengthened in order to guard against any attack on its new owner.

Brecon Castle was built at this position because of its viewpoint over the confluence of the rivers Usk and Honddu respectively, and the fact that any movement on the east-west route between Norman bases could be monitored. Water also provides the power to drive mills and is of course a natural drinking source.

With the castle becoming the administrative military headquarters of the Great Lordship of Brecon, improvements were made and records show these took the form of a polygonal shell constructed on the motte in the 12th Century, and a hall and round tower built in the 13th

century. By the early 14th Century, adjoining the wall on the Honddu side, a semi-octagonal tower was added.

During his time at Brecon Castle, Newmarch was to grant lands and privileges to the monastery which was established as a Benedictine Priory, just to the north of the castle walls where the cathedral stands today.

The charter of c.1100 which Newmarch drew up, also contained a reference to burgages within the castle grounds. These units of land give the indication that the entire settlement was not just geared towards a military function, but towards a civilian community as well.

At the height of its influence on the area, Brecon Castle would have looked very impressive and foreboding.

The main gate faced west overlooking the Usk, and was entered via a drawbridge, then through a portcullis and large door, all overlooked by two semicircular towers, giving near perfect defence. For attack from the town side, a drawbridge too would have stood, exactly on the site of where the current bridge crosses the Honddu today.

A curtain wall enclosed the castle area with the Hall providing the social gathering place, and the residence for the Lord close by in private apartments. The castle also enclosed a chapel and kitchen, plus a 30 feet deep well.

Brecon was to see its fair share of military action. It became a greatly sought after castle, and is recorded as being attacked and captured in 1215; attacked but withstanding in 1231 and 1233; attacked and captured in 1264 and then again in 1265; attacked but withstanding in 1273 and then in 1403, attacked by Owain Glyndwr and his armies.

It was not just the Welsh however that were involved in any fighting with the Normans at Brecon Castle, for it was internal ructions and power struggles involving Kings and their barons, that was to make this a national rather than regional issue.

Owain Glyndwr did however frequent and harass the Normans throughout Breconshire, and two major changes in command of the defence of the castle came. Firstly, with the appointment under Henry IV of Sir Thomas Berkeley to defend it, then one year later, Lord Audley and Lord Warwick were appointed at the castle to quell any threat. For the latter, 100 men-at-arms and 11 mounted archers were enlisted.

Brecon Castle was to pass from Bernard de Newmarch to his daughter Sybil, who married the Earl of Hereford. Their estates in turn passed to William de Braose, remaining in that family for some 100 years. Next to have possession was Humphrey de Bohun through marriage, then it passed into royal hands, before being granted to the Staffords, the last lords of Brecon.

After the demise of the last Lords of Brecon, Acts of Parliament in 1536 and 1543 meant the Marches were brought under royal control. In place of the Lordship of Brecon, the County of Brecknock was born.

With the arrival of Tudors, the age of the castle was in decline and for many years, the Brecon Castle was left to the elements. A survey carried out in 1522, describes how the

roof now leaked and pointed to much of the timber needing replacing.

What we see of Brecon Castle today is mainly due to the Morgan family of Tredegar Park and the time and money they put into restoring it. They went on to turn the adjoining house to the castle into an hotel, the now current Castle Hotel.

BRONLLYS CASTLE

Like many castles sited in the southern Marches, Bronllys Castle is distinguished by its 13th century round keep, standing proud, perched on the top of a steep hill.

Situated 9 miles north east of Brecon, on the A479, Bronllys is amongst a dozen or so castles on the borders of Wales with this design, so constructed as to provide commanding views of the areas around, and to withstand the onslaught of projectiles unleashed from siege engines, which were part of 13th century warfare.

One of the earliest accounts of Bronllys Castle appears in the much quoted Gerald of Wales' "Journey Through Wales", a chronicle of the recruitment mission enlisting soldiers for the Third Crusade.

Gerald refers to Mahel, Earl of Hereford, who was unfortunately present at Bronllys when fire caused damage to its defences. Mahel was struck and killed by a stone. Gerald states that Mahel died full of remorse, believing his fateful encounter with the stone was punishment for Mahel's relentless harassment of the Bishop of St. David's, who happened to be Gerald's Uncle.

The castle construction at Bronllys and indeed all of the these cylindrical tower designs, sprung up during this period in history, as Norman lords set about protecting their land from the disgruntled Welsh, and apart from the 80 ft collosus that stands at Bronllys, another castle with an equally as curious cylindrical tower is that at Tretower in southern Powys, situated 15 miles or so to the south.

Bronllys Castle had two baileys, with a small domestic block being added in the 16th century. Accomodation here was limited, but a nearby church with detached tower would have provided shelter for women and children.

With the Welsh seeking revenge for land lost, these castles served as a priority in this part of Wales, and the structure at Bronllys would have replaced an earlier wooden design, incapable of repelling the ferocity of any attack during the ever changing battle scenarios, where a policy of having stronger, higher and more durable defenses, superseeded anything a much more primitive stronghold could afford.

The lands which were being defended, were given out as a reward for loyal service by Bernard de Neufmarche, following his incursion into Welsh territory. These lands were subsequently set up as lordly manors.

One such supporter of Neufmarch was Richard FitzPons, then baron of Clifford, a village on the English side of the border not far from Bronllys, and he is thought to of seized his land, Cantref Selyf, in the late 1080's, when Neufmarch made an incursion into Brycheiniog.

Therefore we can assume, that the first castle to be built at Bronllys, was most likely the work of Richard FitzPons at the end of the 11th century. It would of been of standard motte and bailey fortification, with an additional rectangular keep. The tower we see today being added much later by Walter de Clifford III, Richard's great grandson. The name Clifford being adopted by Richard's son Walter.

His positioning of the castle afforded views over the junction of two rivers, the Dulais and the Llynfi, giving FitzPons views of any river crossings, on this main route into Welsh territory.

The Clifford family held possession of the castle until the early 14th century, and throughout that time, the castle saw virtually no military action, but along with its counterparts scatterd throughout the region, never the less, played a role in strenghtening hold on the territory, as a collective part of the overall number of fortresses, safety in numbers if you like.

During their occupation, the Cliffords were expected to pay a knight's fee for the castle and any surrounding land under their self imposed authority. There are many other accounts of this 'land duty', whereby you have a sort of landlord and tenant arrangement.

Like all periods in history, being involved in local and national politics had its merits and its pitfalls, and the Cliffords were very active on this scene, with both Walter I and Walter II, fighting against the Welsh in the 12th and 13th centuries.

Walter III also fought the Welsh, under the command of Hubert de Burgh, who owned the 'Monmouthshire Trilateral', three castles forming an important strategic triangle of fortresses guarding the southern March. They comprised White Castle, Grosmont and Skenfrith.

In 1233, the Clifford's support shifted from de Burgh who sided with King Henry III, in favour of Richard Marshal, the rebellious Earl of Pembroke. This cost ownership of the castle when it was seized by the king's forces, but after only a few weeks, control was restored by the Clifford's.

In 1311, the last surviving heir to the Clifford estate, Maud Giffard, died, and within the year, Bronllys Castle came into the ownership of Rhys ap Hywel.

He too had had significant involvement in political matters, costing at one point, his properties and his freedom, with imprisonment.

When he died in 1328, his son Philip ap Rhys took ownership, losing Bronllys however to Humprhey de Bohun IV, who convinced the king that all territory in this part of the Marches should fall under one man's rule, namely him, and so in 1351, he became sole Lord of Cantref Selyf.

Bronllys Castle was to see further changes of ownership, when firstly, following de Bohun's death in 1373, the king took control, then in 1384, it went to Mary, the de Bohun heiress, and her husband Henry, Earl of Derby and son of John of Gaunt. The Duke of Gloucester was having none of this, claiming that Bronllys was Eleanor's, his wife, and the other de Bohun heiress. In 1399 however, Henry, Earl of Derby, was crowned King Henry IV, and all property fell under Crown rule.

During the 15th century, Roger Vaughan of Tretower was appointed custodian of Bronllys Castle by the monarchy, coming into the possession of the Duke of Buckingham in 1478. After his execution for supporting Henry VII, Edward gained ownership, and upon his execution, Bronllys passed back to the Crown.

By 1521, Bronlly was declared "beyond repair', and it wasn't until 1962 that the State intervened to take custody of it. And now, CADW and public support ensure it is preserved for future generations.

CAERPHILLY CASTLE

Situated 9 miles north of Cardiff is Caerphilly, home to the remains of the largest castle in Wales and the second largest castle in Europe, boasting impressive land and water defences, covering in total, a staggering 30 acres.

At twice the size of the Tower of London, this really is a Titan amongst castles, rivalling Windsor in size and ranking as one of the finest examples of military architecture from its period.

The Romans were the first to recognise the strategic qualities of the site, with the erection of a fort around AD 75 for around 500 auxiliary soldiers.

The location is thought to have not been occupied during the early Norman invasion in the late 11th Century, with the conquerors content to concentrate themselves on the more fertile coastal lands, leaving the mountainous uplands to the Welsh.

In effect then, Caerphilly mountain, standing at 889 feet, formed a natural geographical barrier between the Welsh and Anglo-Normans for almost 200 years and in modern times, now forms the divide between Caerphilly town and Cardiff.

It was not until 1268 that construction of the castle we see today started, when Marcher lord Gilbert de Clare - 'Gilbert the Red', began building work to defend his land against attack from the ambitious last Welsh prince of Wales, Llewelyn ap Gruffyd.

Llewelyn at the time controlled Breconshire and was keen to push south into Glamorgan and seize the land there, but upon seeing the imminent threat from Llewelyn, de Clare moved north to make sure upland Glamorgan was secured.

In doing so, he captured the native ruler there, Gruffudd ap Rhys, Lord of Senghennydd, imprisoning him and taking his land.

With construction barely underway,

Llewelyn's forces attacked and burnt the initial works, and only when Llewelyn became distracted by his struggles with Edward I, was building allowed to recommence in 1271.

What was to be built was Britain's first concentric castle, with successive lines of defence set one inside the other, so that attackers having breached one defence, would immediately come up against another, both fatiguing for the arsenal used by the aggressor, and psychologically demoralising too.

De Clare was a wealthy man, who had an estimated income in the region of £5,500 to £6,000 a year. The cost of the castle's construction is put at between £7,500 and £11,000, quite a fair outlay for the wealthiest of people.

It was unlikely that work on Caerphilly Castle was finished by de Clare's death in 1295, with operations being handed over to first his son, also Gilbert, who died at the battle of Bannockburn in 1314, and then to Gilbert's granddaughter, Eleanor and her husband Hugh le Despenser.

In 1316, the castle was again under siege, this time from Llywelyn Bren of Gelligaer, son of the dispossessed Lord of Senghennydd, who had had his lands taken earlier by Gilbert de Clare.

With its formidable defences now at full strength, Llywelyn's men made little inroad, and soon he realised the futility of it all and the fact that fighting on would only harm the cause of his people further. Llywelyn, his wife Lleucu and sons, surrendered to English forces at Castell Coch, and from there imprisonment ensued at King Edward II's command.

Hugh le Despenser, a favourite of the King, then earned the undying hatred of the Welsh by putting Llywelyn to his death in 1318, by having him hung, drawn and quartered in Cardiff.

The ill-fated King Edward II fled to Caerphilly Castle in 1326, in an attempt to evade capture by Queen Isabella. Le Despenser also found himself on the run from a coalition of nobles, eventually being caught and hung, whilst later Edward too was cornered in Llantrisant, and from there taken away and horribly murdered at Berkeley Castle.

The last major military event at Caerphilly Castle was its brief capture by Owain Glyndwr during his revolt at the beginning of the 15th Century, following this, the castle was to steadily fall into decay. To compound its deterioration, it was probably slighted under Cromwell's orders during the Civil War, when the lakes were most likely drained too.

Restoration work was carried out by the 3rd and 4th Marquises of Bute during the 19th and 20th centuries, before guardianship was taken over by the government in 1949.

The castle's overall construction is simply magnificent, and although the actual architect is unknown, the high standard of military engineering and design, and its many similarities with other later concentric castles at Harlech and Beaumaris, point to involvement with that of James of St. George.

The castle is a marvel of defensive visionary, with three distinct wards and seven strong gatehouses in the castle itself and in the outer curtain wall, which formed a formidable barbican.

The inner bailey comprised four towers in a roughly square set-up, incorporating two gatehouses. Each tower and gatehouse protected independently from both the court and the walls by portcullised doorways, giving in total, no less than thirty portcullises in all.

The lower work too was impressively defended by lakes and a fortified dam, making it almost impossible to use many of the normal methods of siege warfare, rendering catapults out of range, siege ladders useless and tunnelling impractical.

Today, one of features most intriguing is that of Caerphilly Castle's leaning tower of the inner ward; a massive piece of 50 foot high masonry, tilting at least nine feet out of perpendicular and out-leaning the world famous Tower of Pisa.

There are various accounts as to why it leans so, including an explosion of steam that blew out the foundations during a siege; an accidental explosion of gunpowder; an unsuccessful Parliamentarian attempt to slight the castle or rather less dramatically of all, subsidence.

Any visitor to the castle will find more than just an impressive ruin. There are many battle re-enactments staged in the grounds, and in the Great Hall, of which Hugh le Despenser is responsible for the rebuilding of, heraldic shields hang amongst the impressive architecture and designs of the time, one of the definite highlights of any visit.

The Castle is open to the public all year round, with visiting times available from either CADW's website, www.cadw.wales. gov.uk, or by telephoning *Caerphilly's Visitor Centre on 02920 883143.*

CALDICOT CASTLE

Situated 5 miles south-west of Chepstow off the B4245, stands the outstanding castle of Caldicot. Restored to much of its former splendour, this medieval fortress has been lovingly cared for by its current owner's and is a real gem to explore in the southern half of Monmouthshire.

Caldicot and the surrounding area has long been recognised for its strategic position. Positioned near the Bristol Channel, any such fortification would have a terrific vantage point to watch all ship traffic across this stretch of water.

The Romans recognised this and made great use of the area in the early centuries of A.D., when Caldicot stood on the Via Julia, a roadway which ran to Caerwent.

It is known that by 49 A.D. most of England was under Roman rule and that legions had pushed as far west to the Severn.

The Roman General Ostorius Scapula had the task of trying to subdue the Welsh tribesmen, as Wales was invaded by the might of the well disciplined and battle eager legions.

As Ostorius tried to consolidate his inroads into Wales by trying to build a camp at Caerleon-on-Usk, the Welsh tribes had mercilessly harried his Roman troops, to the point where Rome itself was becoming angered and bewildered by how these guerrilla outfits could cause such disruption to their forces.

Ostorius was to however fall ill and die and for several years later, Roman plans to invade and conquer Wales were shelved.

Regardless of this, Rome was to still consider at the time, that Wales was another "province" of the Roman Empire, and yet another peaceful settlement of Britain.

The earliest construction on the site at Caldicot Castle was probably built around 1086, and consisted of a motte and two baileys, with a ditch encompassing this early fortification.

When the "Good Earl" of Hereford, Humphrey de Bohun, inherited the Lordship of Caldicot, it was probably he who added the splendid keep in 1221, which boasted four storeys and walls measuring nine feet in thickness and made from local gritstone.

The keep interior indicates that it was used as a residence, though perhaps not one of permanency during that time, rather more of a place to stay on an as and when basis.

Spiral staircases allowed people to pass from one floor to another, whilst inside amongst the fine architectural decor, windows, seats and fireplaces all provided comfort in the style accustomed to the era. Also included in the design, were a latrine, a dungeon and one further chamber.

The tower of course also had its defences which took the form of the current day thinking in military design. These incorporated battlements on the crown of the keep; arrowslits; a wooden fighting platform and at the base of the tower, a splayed plinth.

Caldicot Castle, which remained in the hands of the de Bohuns until 1373 before becoming property of the crown, also added curtain walls, interconnected by round corner towers, all of which enclosed the inner ward.

One of these corner towers was to serve as a secondary residence with accommodation not as grand as the keep, but none the less equipped with a fireplace and two-section window.

It was not until the 14th century that Caldicot's finest feature, the Great Gatehouse, was erected.

Along with the Great Hall which was constructed in the 1340's, the Great Gatehouse has proved to be another building that makes Caldicot Castle such a fine piece of architectural interest today.

Thomas de Woodstock is responsible for the construction of the Great Gatehouse. He had married Eleanor, one of the two daughters who had inherited the Caldicot Castle upon the death of the last male de Bohun. Thomas, was son of King Edward III and Duke of Gloucester, and therefore, the castle was now to pass into royal ownership. Incidentally, Mary de Bohun, the second daughter, married Edward III's grandson, the future King Henry IV.

The Great Gatehouse was to the second gatehouse constructed, one having been constructed earlier and named the West Postern Gate. This was built midway through the 13th century and was defended with a portcullis, a heavy gate and murder holes. This tower proved to be an excellent means of moving persons quickly and covertly away from the castle proper.

The Great Gatehouse however defended the southern face of the castle, and its defences included two portcullises, two heavy gates with access across a drawbridge. Along with three murderholes, this was to prove a much stronger piece of defence work than the first.

With a grand quarters for its residents on the upper floor of the Great Gatehouse, the current occupants of the keep would have now swapped their current dwelling for this new abode, a trend which was coming more to the fore during the Middle Ages in castles of similar set-ups.

Woodstock was to lavish money on the newly acquired castle, setting about undertaking an extensive building project. He was to also add on the north side, the Woodstock Tower, which is a smaller gatehouse in comparison to the Great Gatehouse, but upon which Thomas was to inscribe his wife's name in the masonry, "Alianore".

The Woodstock Tower did however, apart from the customary latrine and window, have a bath, which was quite rare in medieval times.

Unfortunately, Thomas Woodstock died in 1397, so he never really had time to enjoy the massive 'upgrading' plan at the castle. His daughter Anne was to now inherit the castle.

Anne was to marry Edmund, Earl of Stratford and between them they produced a son, Humphrey who in turn inherited the castle, becoming first Duke of Buckingham.

Caldicot Castle then went through a series of owners upon the death of Buckingham during the Wars of the Roses. Firstly to the

Crown, then the Dukes of Stafford, then back to the Crown before eventually ending up in the hands of the Duke of Lancaster.

After falling into disuse, the castle was sold to Victorian barrister Joseph Cobb in 1855. He spent a great deal of time renovating the castle to its former glory.

The castle has subsequently passed into the hands of Monmouthshire County Council.

Today, audio 'Walkman' guides are used in order to give you commentary as you tour the castle and use is still made of the Great Gatehouse, where medieval banquets are held.

Situated in Caldicot town, access to the castle can be gained by leaving the M4 at junction 22. Head for Chepstow, and then the B4245, travelling south west from Chepstow itself, some 4 miles.

CARDIFF CASTLE

Situated in the Welsh nation's capital of Cardiff, lies a truly amazing castle. Just off the main high street stands Cardiff Castle, a real jewel in Wales' crown where the Romans, the Normans and the Victorians have all left their mark, on this splendid fortress.

It is remarkable to think that this site has been in constant occupation from Roman times until 1947, with evidence all around the castle as to who was there, and what they left behind for future occupants.

The first structure here was that of a Roman fort, and comprised a simple ditch and embankment, set on the tidal estuary of the Taff. The present castle we see today follows the outline of that eight-acre walled construction.

The Normans also seeing the strategic importance of such a site, rebuilt on the original framework left by the Romans, turning the old fort into a much more impress defensive stronghold, comprising a motte, crowned with a palisade.

Additional protection came from digging out the original Roman ditch defences and piling the spoil over what remained of the circuit walls, thus creating a rampart.

With the invaders making significant inroads into Wales, Cardiff Castle was the scene of an incredible siege by Welsh forces, under the ruler of Senghennyd, Ifor ap Meurig, when the castle keep was stormed in 1158.

Also known as Ifor Bach, (Little Ivor), this Welsh Lord was chronicled by Gerald of Wales as being 'a man of immense courage, but very short'.

Short or not, he was a determined man with his mind set on stopping the current owner of Cardiff Castle, William de Clare, Earl of Gloucester, from taking more of his land away from him.

The castle was well defended, not only was in crammed full with de Clare's supporters, but had a one hundred strong garrison plus many archers who had a superb field of view from the high walls which they defended.

With the odds seemingly stacked against him,

ladders were brought to the walls and summarily scaled, and in the ensuing chaos, the Earl, his wife and son, were captured and taken away deep into nearby woods, where Whitchurch and Rhiwbeina now stand.

The Normans, having been made to look but an ordinary 'outfit', were forced to meet Ifor's demands in return for the hostages, something the invaders weren't used to. He demanded back the land he'd lost and considerable concessions, which he was duly given.

In the 13th century, the castle first constructed by Robert Fitzhamon around 1081, underwent strengthening improvements, with the erection of the Black Tower, so-called because it housed an unlit, unventilated dungeon, with access only through a trap-door in the Tower's ceiling.

Owain Glyndwr set siege to the castle and town, destroying part of the castle's defences, before in 1425, a great octagonal tower was added, plus a number of domestic dwellings.

Some two hundred years later, the castle changed hands more than once between the Royalists and the Parliamentarians, until eventually the Royalists were defeated at St. Fagan's, some four miles away from Cardiff Castle.

It wasn't until the 18th century that any further building was to take place, when the north wing and the drawing room were added and the octagonal tower gained a spire in 1875.

The guided tour of the castle's interior, which is available to the visitor, will show much of the internal designs dating from the Victorian era and in particular of one architect from this time period, William Burgess.

Burgess transformed the dreams of his patron, John Patrick Crichton Stuart, the third marquess of Bute, into reality.

The work was carried out between 1866 and 1881 and the results of his work are what makes the castle's interior a splendid and memorable period piece; a real slice of flamboyant Victorian architecture of the highest standard.

Money surely couldn't have been a problem, as every satisfaction of the vision of the marquess was met, with the lavishly decorated rooms representing the spirit of medieval romance. Some of them reflecting a certain quaintness of the time, with names like Bachelor's Bedroom and the Chaucer Room.

The collaboration of the marquess of Bute and John Crichton, are best seen in the Clock Tower, the Herbert Tower and the 15th century Octagonal Tower.

Firstly then the Clock Tower, where there is a carved figure of the devil above the arch of the door, leading to the tower. The stairway leads up to the Winter Smoking Room, where the fireplace was hand carved on site, from a block of Forest of Dean stone. The upper parts of the windows display Saxon gods, whilst the ceiling has a central boss representing the sun, surrounded by artwork depicting the twelve signs of the zodiac.

The Bachelor's Bedroom is above, this too boasting ornamental displays, with precious stones inlaid in the stained glass windows

31

and walls. A marble bath adjoins the room, of Roman origin bearing fish designs.

The topmost flight finds the Summer Smoking Room, where a chained dragon guards the entrance, with a bronze model of the world is set in tiles in the centre of the floor.

The Herbert Tower is the most southerly of the projecting towers along the west wall, where the visitor finds a gilded ceiling, cupboards of cedarwood and a chimney-piece of white marble inset with lapis lazuli.

The Octagonal Tower like other towers has a Scottish theme. Firstly, a lion is depicted at the foot of the staircase, and scenes from Aesop's Fables decorate insets on the staircase itself.

The Chaucer Room is at the top of the tower, portraying illustrations from the Canterbury Tales on its stained glass windows, a maze like floor, and a chimney-piece of Milan marble, dominated by the figure of Chaucer himself.

Other parts of the tour will take you to the Banqueting Hall; The Chapel; The Dining Room; The Library and the Entrance Hall, all incorporating the same impressive work.

Today Cardiff Castle holds many events besides guided tours, from private functions to Welsh banquets. The castle is open March to October 9.30 a.m. to 6 p.m., and from 9.30 a.m. until 5 p.m., November to February. Some events may encroach on those time, so before you visit, telephone *(02920) 878100* for the latest information.

Head for the centre of Cardiff. The castle is in Castle Street, to the west of the city centre.

E-mail cardiffcastle@cardiff.gov.uk, or visit the website, cardiffcastle.com

CARREG CENNEN CASTLE

All castles have their defensive attributes, but no matter how good the architect, one particular feature will outweigh any structural piece of building work, and that's the castle's position. One such castle commanding the latter is Carreg Cennen Castle, situated 300 feet high up on a huge rock, overlooking the Cennen valley.

Situated to the north of Swansea, some 4 miles south-east of Llandeilo, this really is a truly magnificent castle, and must have filled any attacker with dread as the castle came into view against the skyline.

The castle stands in the foothills of the Black Mountains and currently resides in privately owned farm land, although access is permitted whilst adhering to the country code. The farm itself has a 17th century longhouse, and has some rare breeds of animal to be observed.

There is only one accessible side to the castle and this can be gained by a steep walk along a slowly rising ridge.

The castle's history is a long one, going back to at least the 13th century, although the discovery of Roman coins and four prehistoric skeletons on the site, suggest dwellers of a much earlier era.

It is the Welsh Princes of Deheubrath that are accredited with building the first castle at

Carreg Cennen, but the first documented piece of evidence regarding a fortress here dates from 1248, whereby one Rhys Fychan had won back the castle following the handing over of it to English hands by his Norman mother, who had carried much hatred for him.

Like with many bitter family feuds of this time, Rhys wasn't to hold on to his castle, being ejected himself by the combined force of Llywelyn, Prince of Wales and Maredudd, Rhy's uncle.

By 1277 the castle was back in English hands under the command of Edward I, who temporarily lost it back to the Welsh in 1282, before regaining it once more.

It was at this point that the castle was granted to John Giffard, who also at this time, had charge of Llandovery Castle.

Giffard set about extensive building work, only to have his efforts interrupted during Maredudd's rising of 1286, when the castle all but fleetingly was captured by the Welsh. They too lost it back to the English, with the Earl of Hereford taking custody of it for two years, before it all came full circle and back into Giffard's ownership.

Whatever the castle may have looked like before this second period of ownership by Giffard was lost forever, as during his sixteen year stay at Carreg Cennen, he transformed it all into more or less of what we see today, leaving very little of what was standing before it.

The castle then past to Giffard the younger who was to then face a serious challenge to his ownership of Carreg Cennen. This came in

the form of Hugh le Despenser, who through marriage and influence over the rather weak king Edward II, became the most powerful baron in South Wales.

He wished to take everything in his path including the Gower, but it was then that a coalition of Marcher Lords, including Giffard, decided enough was enough and tried to put a stop to him.

As a royal favourite, failure was not an option and the king sent forces to make sure the coalition was beaten, which it duly was, and not only did Carreg Cennen Castle become Despenser owned, Giffard the younger was to be executed for standing in his way. Four years later however, Despenser himself was to be executed by the followers of Queen Isabella.

The castle now entered a period where it was to change hands quite frequently. First of all, Henry III granted the castle to Henry of Lancaster, Lord of Kidwelly, who was later to become Duke of Lancaster. In 1362 upon marrying one of the Lancaster heiresses, John of Gaunt acquired the fortress and upon his death it went to his heir, Henry Bolingbroke.

It then became property of the Crown before being attacked in 1403 by Owain Glyndwr's forces, during the second year of his uprising. Uncertainty surrounds whether or not Carreg Cennen was taken by Glyndwr at some point during the rebellion years, varying reports state of it being too much for him to conquer, despite uses of different methods to storm the castle or use a prolonged siege tactic.

During the Wars of the Roses, the castle was held for the House of Lancaster, but following the Yorkist victory at Mortimer's

Cross, all was lost and upon the cessation of hostilities, 500 men were to advance on Carreg Cennen Castle with the intention of slighting it, which duly transpired, rendering it all but useless as a defendable fortress.

Following a further passage of changed ownership, firstly Sir Rhys ap Thomas, then from the 16th to early 19th century by the Vaughan family of Golden Grove, who subsequently bequeathed it to the 1st Baron Cawdor and finally following some attempt to preserve the ruins, to the Department of the Environment in 1932.

Carreg Cennen Castle encapsulates many of the principles of fortification and defence, mirrored in Edward I's castles in north Wales. Predominantly, that of having one set of defences inside another.

The earliest part is the towered inner ward, with a powerful gatehouse incorporating arrow-slits at all levels. The main residential block lies to the left and a chapel in the upper part of a small projecting tower.

Following the construction of the inner ward, a barbican was built which consisted of a long stepped ramp with gates erected to guard it, and pits below moveable bridges.

Last to be built was the outer ward, which extended down the hilltop, incorporating watch-towers at the corners.

One of the castle's most intriguing features however is a narrow vaulted passage, leading down through the south cliff face to a cave below the castle. The passage is bored out of solid rock and lit only by light entering from apertures in the cliff face. The cave was used

in part as a dovecot, being incorporated into the castle's defences to prevent undermining and occupation by attacking forces.

Carreg Cennen Castle is now in the care of CADW, and for further information about this historic fortress, telephone *(01558) 822291.*

CASTELL COCH

If you travel some 6 miles north of Cardiff, off the A470 at Tongwynlais, and gaze upwards at the woods on the hillside, you'll see through the trees the conical turrets of Castell Coch, a fabulous Victorian fantasy for the eye to behold.

Overlooking a gorge in the Taff Valley, Castell Coch is a true marvel and surely one of the most romantic and enchanting buildings in Wales.

Perhaps more in keeping with the Bavarian hillside, or even the studios of Walt Disney, many have seen a quality beyond its walls and have used the location for a number of films, both for the big screen and television.

Two other castles in Wales also share the name, one being a small walled fortification at Ystradfellte in Breconshire, which has mentions in documents dating around 1230.

The other castle being at Marletwy in Pembrokeshire. This Castell Coch was more of a strong house, being constructed in the 15th century.

Surrounded by beech woodland with fields below, it's positioning is perfect and with an exterior of this nature, you wonder could the interior match such standards of excellence?.

Castell Coch is the creation of two men, the extremely wealthy third marquess of Bute and owner of Cardiff's booming docklands, John Patrick Crichton Stuart, and the eccentric but brilliant Victorian architect William Burgess.

These two titans of their time had already set about the rebuilding and transformation of Cardiff Castle, which along with Penrhyn Castle in Bangor Gwynedd, form three of the so-called 'sham' castles built during the 19th century.

These 'sham' castles were built from the fortunes created by the Industrial Revolution, in respect of Cardiff Castle that was coal, and for Penrhyn Castle, slate.

Penrhyn Castle was built by Thomas Hopper for the slate baron G.H. Dawkins Pennant, who drew on the enormous profits of the local quarries for its construction.

Now in the ownership and care of the National Trust, Penrhyn's position in grounds overlooking the Menai Straits, has a distinct air of lavish architecture with its sumptuous looks, rather than a castle built for military use, much the same as Castell Coch.

These castles were a statement, a definite broadcast to surrounding areas and perhaps rivals in the industrial world, a 'solid' expression of new found wealth for all to behold.

However you perceive them and for what reasons, nothing can detract from the fact that all three are stunning, and whether or not the turrets seem too perfect, or the battlements crowned too decoratively, they are in their own right, surviving testimony to that era.

With the marquis settled at his home in Cardiff Castle, he spied Castell Coch as being a companion piece to his first castle, thus further adding to the much talked about speculation, that he was the wealthiest man in the world.

In 1871, the third marquess asked his working partner to carry out a survey and report back with proposals for Castell Coch.

Like Cardiff Castle, the creative genius of William Burgess shone through and the proposal did not disappoint with its highly imaginative reconstruction.

The design was to envisage in its external image, every detail of military construction, being firmly based on medieval precedents, right down to the 'murder-holes', and the portcullis at the castle's entrance.

The site of the castle had been occupied previously, firstly by a short-lived motte and bailey design, erected when the Normans had pushed into the Cardiff area.

The second construction was a more robust stronghold, well-designed and engineered by de-Clare, only lasting a few hundred years however, before being abandoned and deliberately destroyed.

Documentation dating as far back as 1307, talks of 'Rubeum Castrum', which probably referred to this castle and of its red brick, hence Castell Coch, 'Red Castle'.

The plan of this earlier construction would of been roughly triangular, with a round tower situated at each of the angles.

The curtain wall was slightly curved on the longest side opposite the towers, incorporating numerous arrow slits as part of its defences.

Work began on Burges' creation in 1875 and the framework was completed four years later, when suddenly in 1881, the 'eccentric genius' Billy Burgess died, never to see the completion of Castell Coch. It was left to his colleagues to see that his dreams were finished to the splendour he so clearly visualised, right down to the mouldings around the doors, the lavish furnishings and fireplaces.

It took a further 10 years to finish the work and with a strong link to the innards of Cardiff Castle, the completed designs of Burgess are simply amazing, a masterpiece in decorative extravagance.

There is always something to see, with the Dining Room and Keep Tower being the most richly decorated, with the passions of the saints; Aesop's fables; flowers; butterflies; birds and monkeys plus all kinds of other beasts. The splendid vaulted drawing room ceiling is dazzling, not just for the pictured wildlife, but for the shining stars scattered above them.

The Three Fates show that mythology is represented too, these being on the chimney-piece of the drawing room, with further a further mythological depiction in Lady Bute's bedroom, with the winged figure of Psyche.

The bedroom is perhaps the most spectacular, with its domed and mirrored ceiling.

In a further tower, an original well gives its name to the construction within which it lies, which also incorporates steps leading down to a dungeon.

The Kitchen Tower has been set aside to tell the story of the castle, its architect and owner.

Both Cardiff Castle and Castell Coch can be be visited in one day, which will give you full appreciation of the collaboration of the work that went on at both these sites, between the marquis and Burgess.

Now preserved by CADW, Castell Coch is now in the ownership of the Department of the Environment and is open to the public. During the Summer from late March until late October, the castle is opening from 9.30 a.m. until 6.30 p.m., and for other opening times outside of these dates, telephone *(02920) 810101*.

Situated just off the A470 at Tongwynlais, 6 miles north of Cardiff.

CHEPSTOW CASTLE

Situated high above the River Wye to the north end of the town of Chepstow, stands the mighty and impressive Chepstow Castle, guardian of one of the main crossing points from southern England into Wales.

Work on Chepstow Castle was started back in 1067 by William FitzOsbern, Norman

Lord of Breteuil, and following the Battle of Hastings, made earl of Hereford by William the Conqueror. William was given the task of quietening any unrest from the Welsh in the southern borderlands and through aggressive means, managed to ultimately encompass Chepstow, as he pushed his Hereford border westwards.

During the construction by FitzOsbern, he incorporated a long rectangular fortified hall, (the Great Tower), on the narrowest part of the ridge overlooking the Wye. The Great Tower was built as a two storey structure, featuring a string course of Roman tiles, thought now to have been robbed from the ruins of Caerwent. To protect his Great Tower, FitzOsbern built a stone curtain wall on all four sides. It is the earliest datable secular stone building in Britain, very similar to other 11th century stone keeps sited in Normandy.

The Castle was separated from the town by a deep gully, known as the 'Dingle'.

After his death, the earldom of Hereford, including Chepstow Castle, now became entrusted to his son, Roger of Breteuil. It was taken out of his hands in 1075, following involvement in a failed rebellion against William I, for which he was imprisoned.

In 1115, the castle passed into the hands of Walter FitzRichard of the powerful Clare family. Henry I had granted it to FitzRichard along with a huge area of land to create the lordship marcher of Striguil, the old Welsh name for Chepstow, meaning "the bend", as the River Wye bends as it passes the town.

FitzRichard made no structural alterations to Chepstow Castle, his name mainly being remembered as the founder of Tintern Abbey.

Upon his death and with no heir, Chepstow passed through several ownership changes, until William Marshall, Earl of Pembroke, inherited it through marriage. Marshall was famous as an outstanding soldier of fortune, and using his vast knowledge of military architecture, set about bringing Chepstow Castle up to date. He rebuilt the east curtain wall, with two round towers, incorporating arrow-slits, to give covering fire to the ground directly outside the curtain.

Henry III is chronicled to have stayed at the Castle in the summer of 1217, two years before the death of Marshall in 1219.

The castle was now in the hands of Marshall's five sons, who set about continuing their father's work. Apart from the construction of a barbican and additions to the Great Tower, they added a new lower bailey with a twin-towered gatehouse.

Following the five sons deaths, all of whom were childless, the Castle became ownership of Maud, eldest of William Marshall's five daughters. Her son Roger Bigod II took no interest in the Castle, but his son, Roger Bigod III certainly did.

Bigod set about making yet more improvements to the Castle, and between 1270-1300, made his mark as one of the greatest magnates of his day. Included in an impressive list of modifications to the Castle were the addition of a western gatehouse; a vaulted cellar; construction of the 'Port' or town wall; a latrine built high over the river cliff and a whole range of domestic buildings in the lower bailey.

Another splendid addition is that of which was later to be called, Marten's Tower, a massive 'D' shaped structure enabling flank fire across invaders attempting to penetrate the barbican and also incorporating Bigod's private residence.

Marten's Tower was so-called after the regicide Henry Marten who was imprisoned in it. Marten had been one of the signatories to the death warrant of Charles I, but was spared death following the restoration of Charles II, because of his unwavering belief that Cromwell really did want to be crowned King of England.

The next owner of Chepstow Castle was John, Roger's brother. Edward I was next in possession followed by Hugh le Despenser, who set about carrying out his own repairs. It changed hands again but Despenser bought the Castle back in 1323, only to surrender it without siege in 1326.

It wasn't until the revolt of Owain Glyndwr, that Chepstow Castle again became involved in military affairs. By 1403, there was a garrison of 60 archers and 20 men-at-arms, which was enough to deter any attempt to overthrow the Castle.

Following the execution of its then current owner, Thomas Mowbray, Duke of Norfolk, the Castle went to William Herbert, Lord Raglan and Earl of Pembroke.

The Castle entered a relatively quiet period until the outbreak of Civil War when the owner at the time, Henry, 5th Earl and 1st Marquis of Worcester, was embroiled in the events between the warring factions of the Parliamentarians and the Royalists.

As an ardent Royalist, the Marquis held the Castle in the name of Charles I, but an expected Parliamentarian attack from their Monmouth garrison on the Castle never came, as a Royalist attack on them first made them think twice.

During the second Civil War, Oliver Cromwell personally oversaw an attack on Chepstow Castle which was being defended by the valiant Sir Nicholas Kemeys and 120 men. Cromwell's guns smashed the walls of the castle, which had only been designed against medieval attack. As members of Kemey's army fled and surrendered, believing the cause was lost, the courageous Nicholas fought on, eventually dying sword in hand. Before the Castle had even fallen, Cromwell had already left and was heading westwards towards Pembroke.

When the Civil Wars ended, the whole southern face of the castle was reinforced so that cannon fire could be withstood. The parapets were remodelled with musket loops.

The ownership had by now passed from Cromwell, who was granted it at the end of hostilities, to Lord Herbert, son of the rightful owner.

The Castle then went on to be used as a prison, holding Henry Marten, of which the tower was renamed, until 1690 when orders were given to dismantle it. That never really took place as the resident garrison had left the Castle.

Ownership was then passed down to Henry's successors, eventually being sold to a Mr W.R. Lysaght in 1914.

Today, the Department of the Environment

own Chepstow Castle, having been given permanent guardianship of it in 1953.

Access off the M4 travelling up from Cardiff at junction 23, or junction 2 off the M48. From Bristol, junction 21. Numerous car parks all within walking distance of the castle, which is situated to the north end of the town, overlooking the River Wye. Tel (01291) 624065.

COITY CASTLE

Situated to the north-east of Bridgend stands the majestic ruin of Coity Castle, centre of an important Norman Lordship and a much besieged fortress during the Welsh uprising of Owain Glyndwr.

The initial stronghold was built by Payn de Turberville and was no more than an earthen 'ringwork', with a timber palisade, crowning the bank and encompassed by a circular ditch. The dating of this initial work is non-specific but if certain legends are true, then it would of been constructed in the early to mid 1100's.

One particular legend often quoted, is that regarding Payn de Turberville himself. Payn was one of eleven knights given land by Robert Fitzhamon, who played a significant part in the Norman conquest of Glamorgan.

Fitzhamon, perhaps better known as the founder of Cardiff Castle around 1081, decided that as a reward for their services, the knights should be given some land each.

Payn however wasn't given land, just a

number of men and arms, and with it, the free will to take what land he desired.

His journey brought him to Coity Castle and upon his arrival he liked the look of the place so much, he demanded that the Welsh Chieftain then resident there, named Morgan, surrender it all immediately to him without fail. Morgan's answer was to ride out to meet Payn ready for battle, accompanied by his not-unattractive daughter Sybil.

Payn was then given a choice by the Chieftain. He could fight there and then with him in a personal duel or marry Sybil and inherit Coity. Payn handed his sword to Morgan with his left hand, holding it by the blade and with his right arm, embraced the Chieftain's daughter.

After he was wed, Payn swore allegiance to Caradoc ap Jestyn and moved into Coity Castle with his new family, all of which was defended by a great force of Welshman, supplied with Morgan's aid.

There may be anomalies in the legend, but it is true that Payn was in Glamorgan until at least 1126 and that his descendants are chronicled as having lived at Coity Castle until the end of the 14th Century, when the male line of the Turbervilles became extinct.

As far as Coity Castle itself goes, it was probably Gilbert de Turberville who converted the defences into stone, incorporating a powerful stone keep and a curtain wall following the line of the bank.

Upon the Turberville line ending, Coity Castle and its estates were divided up and it passed much later on into the ownership of Sir William Gamage. It was around this time that much structural redevelopment was done to the Castle, and with some division in the history books, the name Sir Lawrence of Berkerolles becomes associated with much of the remodelling, even suggesting that it was he before Sir William Gamage who had ownership of Coity when the work was done.

Coity's list of improvements include the introduction of a stone wall to reinforce the outer ward, including square towers at the angles; a new tower was added to the south of the keep, and a middle gate built in place between the two, also a chapel and hall constructed against the curtain of the inner ward. The east gate was to get a drawbridge and portcullis.

By 1400, the name of Owain Glyndwr, 'The Welsh Prince' was becoming prominent throughout the land and it was at Coity that a prolonged siege was to take place. As Owain attacked Glamorgan, Coity stood as one of the many castles in the county that had to be taken.

Owain's army, or as they were more widely becoming known, 'Owain's Children', had already instigated attacks to the north at Ruthin, Denbigh, Flint, Hawarden, Holt and Rhuddlan, besieging both fortress and town at each encounter.

By all accounts, Coity Castle appears to have withstood Owain's onslaught, but not before the length of siege had aroused concerns in the House of Commons, who requested that Henry IV, oversee the removal of Lord Coity from the Castle.

Details of Owain Glyndwr's campaign strategy during the revolt is unclear. There is little to speak of about an overall plan, distribution of forces bar anything more than fireside rumour. It is said that as he led the Welsh in gaining their independence as a Welsh nation from outsiders, he was uncannily elusive, so much so, that he and his men would simply melt away into the background when trapped or outnumbered.

It is true however that Henry never engaged Owain's forces in a decisive battle. As a guerrilla leader, Owain Glyndwr's disruptive tactics across Wales were first rate, so much so, that all the kings money, time and expeditions into Wales to stop him were virtually fruitless.

Owain was to become more than a guerrilla leader though, taking on the stance of a diplomat and indeed something of a statesman.

Thereby goes another wonderful legend. Tales of Owain would be referred to later by Shakespeare's Henry IV, with talk of his mystical ability to conjure up the likes of spirits and storms, in fact possessing powers of a wizard and the ability to inhabit other bodies to his own. All of this fuelling the fears within his enemies and sparking the inspiration to rise up and fight within the Welsh.

Owain had indeed instilled a spirit in the Welsh, and when a great army of Henry's which advanced on Wales from three bases was driven back by torrential rain storms and high winds, the legend was further fuelled.

When the male line of the Gamages ended at the end of the 16th Century, Coity Castle came into the ownership of Sir Robert Sidney, following his marriage to Barbara Gamage in 1584. Sir Sidney later went on to be second Earl of Leicester.

It wasn't until Tudor times that Coity Castle saw any further work. The moat, which originally encircled the whole inner ward was filled in where it ran through the outer ward. There was the addition of third storey to the hall block and a four floor annexe added to the north-west side of the Castle's keep. This was to be the last work carried out at the Castle.

Today Coity stands abandoned and has been so since the late 16th Century.

Situated 2 miles north-east of Bridgend, take the A4061 for Coity.

CYFARTHFA CASTLE

Merthyr Tydfil was once known as the 'iron and steel capital of the world' during the days of the Industrial Revolution, and whoever may of been in position of power at the time, could quickly reap the benefits of such a dynamic age in global history.

In this case, one such man commanding 'Ironmaster' status was William Crawshaw who commissioned the building of Cyfarthfa Castle in 1824, constructing it to reflect the wealth and prosperity of the era, and sending out a clear message to rivals and allies alike, a stone built mansion saying "I have achieved!".

Situated one mile north west of the town centre, off the A470, Cyfarthfa stands as Castell Coch just outside Cardiff does today, testimony to lavish architecture and construction of the highest order, emanating wealth and the ability via construction, to let one's imagination take hold, and let the creative mind know no bounds, in producing a masterpiece.

Like a small proportion of castles, Cyfarthfa today is not just a castle to visit and admire, it is place whereby other attractions are incorporated to make the visitors day a more entertaining one, which in essence is the way forward in this modern world where "needs must", but I do encourage you upon visiting, to not forget the root of all you see there, for it is the castle that sparks the initial desire for interest.

That spark has a history, for back in 1750, Merthyr Tydfil was no more than a village settlement, but by 1801, it had grown by a huge extent, like the 'boom towns' that sprung up during the 'Gold Rush' decades in America's history.

In Wales though it wasn't the eye catching, glittery attraction and rich rewards of gold, it was iron, and although no where near as enticing as a glint in prospector's pan, it was neither 'fool's gold' either.

For iron was big business, and soon powerful dynasties were emerging from the Valleys, in the form of the Guest family, the Homfray family and the Crawshaws.

In this great time, there was always going to be the people who capitalised on the current situation, seeing potential and reaping the rewards of the moment. Indeed, throughout the ages, there has always been a man or woman for the moment, an opportunist who will seize the day, and for the men of iron, that time was now.

These families were to control the four great ironworks that had sprung up during the period, at Cyfarthfa itself, with the others being at Dowlais, Penydarren and far away Plymouth, which was distant enough to not cause any problems to the men from the Valleys, but on a global scale, still be a competitor for trade none-the-less.

If you can envisage it, from quiet village to noisy, round the clock iron production, where the Merthyr night sky would glow bright, as the furnaces smelted metal which would be sent world-wide to as far flung places as Siberia, where it would be laid as rail track.

Whilst the 'Ironmasters' gorged the benefits of the age, the workers would simply work, and work and work, with employment being the only reward for them. Their homes were the small, crammed, terraced houses, whilst Crawshaw was to have his castle built for all to see, creating a brickwork fortress for himself, and forever instilling a 'them' and 'us' attitude between worker and employer.

Cyfarthfa Castle was raised in just one year, 1824 to 1825, and was called 'the most impressive monument of the Industrial Iron Age in southern Wales'. It overlooked Crawshaw's own ironworks which had now become the largest in Britain. The workers would endure its presence as they trudged back and fore to work.

William Crawshaw himself was a man of extravagance, a colourful character who would entertain many a guest of the Victorian age with lavish hospitality and outside of iron production, was extensively involved with photography, indeed the museum at the castle has many interesting exhibits.

The castle stands in a landscaped 65 hectare, (160 acre), parkland, overlooking a part of Merthyr which contains Chapel Row. The visitor can see Chapel Row and upon doing so, will understand the void between the classes, as Chapel Row was preserved to show just how the workers lived in these purpose built houses for the iron workers.

Such was the divide, it was to make an impact on the political scene, for in 1900, Merthyr became the first town in Britain to elect a Socialist MP to Parliament, one Keir Hardie.

At this point, upon the subject of discussing firsts, putting the record straight is something else Merthyr historians would also like to make clear.

For it was Cornishman Richard Trevithick behind the pioneering railway system, which ran from Merthyr to Abercynon in 1804, a full 20 years before Stephenson's 'Rocket' laid any claim. A monument to the feat serves as a reminder at the top of the High Street.

Like all eras of boom and bust, matters do come full circle and it was the introduction of the Bessemer process, revolutionising the iron industry, that was to see the demise of the 'Ironmasters'.

Cyfarthfa Castle seems to encapsulate 'ruggidness' as its main outward design quality, ignoring the more cleaner lines of Classical architecture. The battlement towers and false arrow-loops are a reminder of the medieval baronial past.

Today, the visitor will find much to entertain, with the main suite of state rooms serving as a museum and art gallery and whilst that baronial theme is reflected in the entrance hall, there is a strong Classical influence in the style and surroundings of the library, dining room, and drawing room.

You'll also find Cafe 'Bardi' within the museum, which pays homage to the South Wales Valley's Italian communities.

For anyone making a journey from outside the area, take the M4 motorway to junction 32, then travel north on the A470 to Merthyr Tydfil, and follow the details mentioned earlier. In fact, Cyfarthfa Castle is an easy walk from the town centre, or indeed a bus service will take you to the castle's gates.

Admission is free, with varying opening times throughout the year. For details telephone *(01685) 723112* or email for help, questions and news on the many events there, museum@cyfarthfapark.freeserve.co.uk

DINEFWR CASTLE

The majority of castles that were built with more than just a statement of being wealthy, or using decorative work to emulate a past era, are built to hold and defend territory. One of the best pieces of strategic building to do just that, is Dinefwr Castle.

One has to only to look at the great circular keep, to be reminded of similar ones situated at Skenfrith in Monmouthshire, and Tretower Castle in Powys. A prominent and daunting creation, steeped with power and influence, with commanding views across the countryside.

There is a definite bone of contention as to what lay on the site of the castle, before the fortress as we know it today was built. Suggestions of a possible prehistoric fortification has little support, and further talk of Roman influence here early on, is too confined to conjecture, despite numerous finds of Roman material in areas nearby.

The site is also reputed to date back to 876

A.D., and Rhodri the Great. It was Rhodri who divided the kingdom of Wales into three, with Gwynedd as the north; Powis as the central land and Deheubarth as the south. Rhodri's decision to do so would from that moment on, reshape not just the layout of the land, but influence history for hundreds of years to come.

It is supposed that in doing so Rhodri envisaged greater peace throughout the kingdom, alas, this was not to be.

The Welsh lawbooks of the medieval period, afford Dinefwr Castle special status, as the principal court of the kingdom of Deheubarth, on a par with that of Aberffraw, chief court of the kingdom of Gwynedd.

Situated one mile west of Llandeilo, Dinefwr Castle stands high on a wooded cliff-top, overlooking the River Tywi, and like neighbouring Carreg Cennan Castle, would of commanded great respect from any invader, thinking of scaling its defences. Dinefwr's defensive ditches being cut from solid rock.

History of the castle shows that a considerable number of people who owned Dinefwr Castle, were name Rhys.

For in 12th century, one of the greatest Welsh leaders was Rhys ap Gruffydd, who withstood an onslaught not just by the Anglo-Norman lords of the March, but Henry II's forces too, ensuring that Deheubarth flourished under his patronage and governance, having dispensed with would-be deposers to his lofty position.

Rhys over the next two decades brought a large part of the former kingdom under his control and in doing so, reversed the fortunes

of the Welsh kingdom as a whole, relieving the great pressure imposed by the English.

We cannot be entirely sure as to what sort of fortress he had at Dinefwr, but all the pointers are to what the visitor sees of it today. The castle that the first lord Rhys occupied was dismantled in 1220, but the late 12th century wards are still traceable now. The keep was added in the 13th century, with domestic buildings dating from some one hundred years later.

Following the death of Rhys ap Gruffydd in 1197, his succession to the kingdom of Deheubarth was bitterly contested, by his eldest legitimate son, Gruffydd ap Rhys, Maelgwyn ap Rhys and Rhys Gryg. A struggle ensued that was continue even after Gruffydd ap Rhys' death, with his sons carrying on the feud.

Eventually a settlement was reached in 1216, when the prince of Gwynedd, Llywelyn ap Iorwerth, stepped in a used his power to create three separate divisions within Deheubarth, in a way resolving the matter, but in doing so, lessening the kingdom's strength.

Other notable times in the castle's 'war log' include 1287, when another Rhys captured the castle back from the English after Edwards' campaigns, also, Dinefwr surviving an attack from Owain Glyndwr's forces in 1403, when much damage was done, but the castle remaining uncaptured.

Construction at Dinefwr Castle stemmed from the initial 13th century building work, with the keep surviving from early in that period, situated in the inner ward, and parts of the curtain wall, also surviving from around the 1230's.

The keep and adjacent Welsh gate have been attributed to Rhys Gryg, who during a time of peace in Deheubarth, was able to concentrate on building operations. There may be some doubt as to whether the work is his, but a very similar construction at nearby Dryslwyn Castle, seems too much of a coincidence.

Following his death and after the Edwardian conquest, further work including repairs to the tower and bridge were carried out, and the ditches cleared and further extended to incorporate other buildings.

There are also references to a 'little tower' around this time, which was probably built during the repair work, and seems to refer to the north-west tower, which underwent remodelling at this time.

In addition, a rectangular chamber block was constructed, to the north-east of the castle, incorporating a watch turret.

Furthermore, the creation of an inner gate and barbican, incorporating a southern turret.

As we push on through the years, comfort and space seemed to take precedence over everything else, when considerable amounts of money were spent during the Hakelut's custody, around 1326, with the addition of a rectangular hall and another structure along the western curtain.

Despite there being evidence pointing to some refurbishing taking place at the turn of the 15th and 16th Centuries, generally, it seems that few further repairs were carried out until the 17th Century, and even despite this, fire was destroy any maintenance work and by the 18th century the castle was abandoned.

Throughout the 20th century some maintenance work has been undertaken by the Dinefwr Estate, and at present, subsequent repair work is ongoing.

Today, Dinefwr Castle in not fully open, due to the restoration work, so a telephone call to Dinefwr Park would be advisable, to find out just what can be seen.

Dinefwr Park is set in glorious woodland and is a National Trust landscape, laid out by Capability Brown, in the 18th century. There is also the Castle Woods Nature Reserve, a 62 acre sanctuary based around the south and west slopes of the castle. Access to the castle can be gained through Dinefwr Park.

Head for Llandeilo, and the castle is situated 1 mile to the west of the town.

G

GOODRICH CASTLE

Standing on a high spur overlooking the River Wye is the splendid Goodrich Castle, a prominent fortress situated on the Welsh Marches to the north of Symonds Yat, impregnable on two sides due to the cliff faces, and protected on the landward side by a moat.

Goodrich Castle can be found off the A40 road, some seven miles away from the town of Monmouth if travelling out of Wales, and four miles south west of Ross-on-Wye in Herefordshire.

Goodrich Castle was built up over several phases with the Fitz Baderons starting work on the structure, followed later by the de Valences who made many additions to the earlier work.

Research indicates that the first family involved, the Fitz Baderons, were classed as a lower noble family, as they possessed only one keep, suggesting that, they weren't higher up in the nobility chain, than the first rung, so to speak.

The de Valences however were a more powerful family altogether, and the additions that they were to make to Goodrich show the increased need and provision of ostentation, and as with all structures both old and new, the more lavish the look, the more it speaks of wealth, power and money.

The earliest surviving work at Goodrich is the keep, dating from the mid-twelfth century, 1160 to 1170. It consists in its form, three rooms situated on top of each other, standing 25 by 25 square feet, (and deemed when clasing keeps of this time period, in comparsion to that of Goodrich's), a small keep. It has to be said though none the less in affording the construction of one at all, lower, middle or higher nobility, in my opinion, it's still a keep.

The Fitz Baderons had the original entrance to the keep situated up a flight of external stairs, which led to the floor doorway.

Such a design would of served as a form of defence, be it all just adequate enough to hold any intruder at bay temporarily, but in the 14th and 15th Century, this was to be blocked off and the door entrance moved to the ground floor, indicating a change in thinking away from using such access as being defensible.

Within the keep itself, a staircase situated in the north west corner would give access from the first floor to the second floor, and from this, onto the roof. A trap door would provide access to the basement below.

Further research supports the idea that once again the Fitz Baderons were a poor noble family. This is reached at by discovering that the keep does not hold the chapel and hall, which both lay in the courtyard area. This indicates that they could not afford such features along with any other expense that was to be incurred in the building of the castle, something modern day architects may look upon as minimalism if you like, or working to a budget.

Buttresses at the angles of the keep walls served as defences, with the buttress central to each of the flat sides, providing cover from any catapult shot fired from the ground beneath.

Other notable defensive positions include the 14th Century barbican and drawbridge, which would have forced any attacker to take on not one but two bridges, before having to assail the gate, therefore providing more of a deterrent than anything else.

All castles throughout the world fit into a model design, with the architecture and construction reflecting the period, the builders and owners, not to mention giving an insight into whether or not that part of history in which it was built, was one of peace or one of turbulence. Many Welsh castles reflect the marks of Owain Glyndwr's campaign and registering for all to see, the impact one man can make on history.

Goodrich Castle fits into one particular category too, one which incorporated earlier motte and bailey sites with a basic military requirement in its construction thinking, but then taken by subsequent owners and developed for more spatial purposes, hence the 'make over' if you like, impressing their blueprint for expansion and change and inherently incorporating three aspects that were

then deemed priority, the keep, courtyard, and gatehouse.

Goodrich Castle's gatehouse was built around 1300, and is housed in the north east tower of the castle. The gatehouse consists of a 50 foot long vaulted corridor with a portcullis barring it at each end, with a vaulted chamber opening out to provide access to the lower areas of the tower itself.

The chapel lies in the upper part of the tower, absent from the keep. This chapel would of served the garrison and we know this because the stairs in the north east tower led to the portcullis room, meaning the Lord would of been in a separate part of the castle, away from a potentially 'vulnerable' position, which this would of been deemed.

The 70 foot courtyard at Goodrich was used to a greater extent because of the castle's small keep, housing more non defensible facilities than perhaps was practical, as most of these would of been situated in a higher status keep, or indeed the Great Hall.

The de Valences later addition of the Great Hall measuring 65 by 27 feet, included the private chambers, an entrance to the Solar, (sitting room), and a private chapel. We can attribute a lot of this later construction to Henry III's half-brother, William de Valence, Earl of Prembroke, altogether being responsible for the rectangular inner ward, the gatehouse and the three angle drum towers.

In 1326 Goodrich was successfully beseiged and subsequently destroyed by Parliamentary troops during the English Civil War.

And so, a tale of two families and perhaps

two classes with a divide between what one would like to have built, and what one could afford to have built.

In fact, when visiting Goodrich, it is also a perfect opportunity to take in several more castles which are to be found nearby. There is the magnificent Raglan Castle, just off the A40 in the small village of the same name, and en-route towards Goodrich from Wales, Monmouth Castle, with strong family links to Goodrich Castle itself through the Fitz Baderon family, and birthplace of future king, Henry V, victor at Agincourt.

Goodrich Castle is open daily, April to September, 10 a.m. to 6 p.m., and during October 10 a.m. until 5 p.m., and November to March, 10 a.m. until 4 p.m. For further information contact English Heritage on *(01600) 890538.*

Goodrich Castle is positioned to the north of Symond's Yat. It is situated 4 miles off the A40, travelling south-west from Ross-on-Wye, or north-east from Abergavenny.

Grosmont Castle

Brecon Castle

Ogmore Castle

Caerphilly Castle

L

LAUGHARNE CASTLE AND WEOBLEY CASTLE

Standing tall overlooking the Taff estuary lies Laugharne Castle, an imposing feature against the skyline, and a true stone guardian against any aggressor.

Situated off the A4066 from St. Clears, 9 miles south-west of Carmarthen, the castle is sited next to the Coran stream, on a low cliff, that overlooks the expanse of the estuary.

Laugharne Castle must share its stature with a very famous Welshman, poet, writer and one time resident Dylan Thomas. Thomas lived in 'The Boathouse', standing on the banks of the estuary. Needless to say, a trip to the town of Laugharne wouldn't be complete without a visit there, even if the motive for going was to look at the castle.

It is thought that Laugharne Castle may have been the castle mentioned in a document of 1116, as being in the ownership of Robert Courtemain, but this evidence is inconclusive.

There is a definite reference however to the castle in 1189, when it was seized from Norman hands after the death of King Henry II, by Lord Rhys, Prince of Deheubarth.

This particular time in history marks a turbulent period for the castle, as it was repeatedly taken by the Welsh from the Normans, who subsequently took it back on each ocasion. From the records, we can see that this changing of owners went on for many years, up until the second part of the 13th Century.

Documentation points to the castle being destroyed by the Welsh in 1215 by Llewellyn The Great, before it's recapture of what remained by the Normans, then being taken in 1257 and burnt by Welsh forces.

The first well-established owner of Laugharne Castle was Sir Guy de Brian, who took residence in the early 14th Century. The connection with de Brian and the castle, at last marked some stability for Laugharne.

Archaeological work on the castle in recent times, traces what remains of the site back to de Brian, with only fragments of a building with a large hearth, pointing to work prior to his occupation.

A hill fort may well have stood there initially, while local traditions claim that it was the site for the marriage of King Arthur to Guinevere.

From the de Brians and their descendants, the castle passed to earls of Northumberland in 1488, and then in 1584, Elizabeth I granted Laugharne to Sir John Perrott, said to be the illegitimate son of Henry VIII.

Despite much work on making the castle defensible by Guy de Brian, the fortress fell into decline following his death in 1390, and it wasn't until Sir John Perrott's reign of ownership came, that any further substantial alterations were made.

Perrott, an important dignitary, set about converting the old medieval castle into a Tudor mansion, with mock battlements, a large accommodation block and the raising of the inner gatehouse to a more impressive height.

Sadly for Perrott however, the Royals began to look unfavourably on him, deeming that he had become too powerful in their eyes, and subsequently in 1592 he was sentenced to death for high treason.

Perrott though died of natural causes before any such punishment could be administered.

Much later in 1644 during the Civil War, Laugharne was captured by Royalists supporters, who held the castle for a time, before Roundhead forces claimed it as theirs.

The ravages of war had left its mark on the castle and with it standing partially destroyed following conflict, it fell into gradual disrepair.

For any visitor today, the substantial ruins consist of an outer ward, it's diamond-shaped curtain wall, with a gatehouse on the north side.

The inner ward consisting of two large round towers and part of the inner gatehouse, represent the de Brian input to the castle.

The hall block standing between the two towers was added during Tudor times, with Perrott constructing a second hall against the south curtain.

Besides the attraction of Dylan Thomas who described the castle as as "brown as owls", Laugharne also lured JMW Turner to paint the fortress in watercolour. Richard Hughes, author of 'A High Wind in Jamaica', also wrote here.

For more information on Laugharne Castle call (01994) 427906. The castle is open for visiting from 10 a.m. to 5 p.m., May to September.

More spectacular views can be had from Weobley Castle, situated near Llanrhidian, on the Gower Penninsula, 7 miles west of Gowerton and some 11 miles west of Swansea.

It is believed that the de la Bere family first held the sub-lordship of Weobley back in the early part of the 12th Century, following the Norman conquest of the Gower area.

David de la Bere is considered likely to have started work on the late 13th Century buildings, with John de la Bere being the last documented 'la Bere' holding the castle in 1432, with no subsequent entries with the family name being recorded later.

Also, research uncovers that the castle was meant to be much bigger than what was finally achieved, and strictly speaking, Weobley is not so much a castle, more a fortified manor house, and not a particularly strong one at that.

Having said this, the castle, as I prefer to call it, does give us well preserved insight into the domestic arrangements in such a building towards the end of the Middle Ages.

The most substantial remains of the buildings which show some of the arrangement layout, are grouped around a small open courtyard.

On the north side stands the hall, situated on the first floor, with the kitchens below. A great fireplace warmed the hall, with a window lighting the high table where the family sat for meals. Near the window, a door led to the solar, or private accommodation, whilst on the other side of the hall, a first floor guest chamber can be found.

A square structure to the south of the courtyard served as a 'tower house', with a chapel next to it on the first floor. The east side was never finished.

Following attacks from Owain Glyndwr's forces, Sir Rhys ap Thomas was the only resident to make further intended alterations in the 15th Century, adding a porch block, only later to be modified in the 16th Century for domestic use, then eventually, into a tenant farmhouse.

After several more ownership changes, the guardianship came to rest with the Government in 1911.

Weobley Castle is situated at Llanrhidian, near Gowerton. Off the Llanrhidian-Cheriton road, 11 miles west of Swansea.

LLANSTEFFAN CASTLE

There's little more encapsulating of Welsh legends than to see a beautiful castle perched high on a cliff top, overlooking the seemingly never ending expanse of countryside. One such castle that evokes such an image is Llansteffan Castle, as it imposes itself over Carmarthen Bay, with views stretching to the western tip of the Gower Peninsula.

Situated on the headland some 8 miles south west of Carmarthen itself, lies this splendid fortification, which has been a defended position since prehistoric times.

It's not difficult to imagine just why the site was picked, as high on a bluff fronting the sea, it is in fact a small peninsula formed by the Gwendraeth, Towy and Taf rivers.

Your start point will be in the pretty village of Llansteffan, ("the church of Stephen"), situated below, which includes some idyllic houses and shops.

From the southern end of main car park, you make your way up the steep hillock at the base of the fortress, where pathways will take you to the castle.

Llansteffan Castle may not be one of the most important of Welsh castles, but the individuality of its construction, coupled with the people who were in residence there, make it none the less an integral part of our history, offering something vital to the overall jigsaw.

There is evidence at the front of the castle, just before the gatehouse, that people from the Iron Age made use of the site.

Visible in the bracken and trees are the remains of earthworks, which would give more than good reason to believe a fort stood there.

This would have been an Iron Age promontory fort, occupied as far back as 6th century BC.

Further more powerful earthworks were built to form the oval Upper Ward, also a large outer bailey. It's refortification as a Anglo-Norman stronghold also involved the Iron Age ditches being recut and construction of a so-called 'ringwork' castle of earth and timber, being constructed within.

Stonework was to eventually enclose the whole area and the Upper Ward was revetted in masonry in the late 12th century, or early part of the 13th century.

A square gatehouse was also an addition to its construction, followed by a mid to late 13th century wall, which was built around the entire outer ward, with two round towers and a bastion on the eastern corner also erected.

Leaving possibly the best until last is the massive double-towered gatehouse, which is today's main access point for visitors.

Its design is based on that of the one at Caerphilly Castle, though perhaps not with the same stature. This was however walled up in the late 15th century with a smaller entrance made in the wall alongside it.

In its time however it was the main residence at the castle, and was later converted to a Tudor house. The original construction boasted protection from portcullises, and 'murder-holes'

above. There was also a chute made over the front arch, from which boiling liquids could have been poured on any attackers below.

In 1093 the Normans arrived on our shores, in what we now know as Carmarthenshire. Resistance from the feisty Welsh was stiff and unwavering and it took the invaders 13 long years to take this part of Wales.

It wasn't until 1146 that Llansteffan Castle was captured by the Welsh, under the guidance of three princes of south Wales, Maredudd, Rhys and Cadell, this following a successful assault at Carmarthen Castle.

The Welsh record of castle defences is especially patchy when it comes to ladder assaults, but it is recounted that one of the princes, Maredudd, became a hero when he despatched an assault of this nature at Llansteffan, hurling the ladders of the attackers down into the ditches below.

Before the princes took the castle, there are some references to an early raid being carried out at Llansteffan in 1137, however these are not clear as they may in fact relate to Castell Stephan near Lampeter, and not Llansteffan at all.

The castle remained in Welsh possession for the next 12 years, until the Normans regained control, only to then lose it again to the Welsh under the direction of Lord Rhys of the South, who had broke with the English when Richard I became king in 1189.

The castle was soon lost and this time it fell into the hands of the monarchy, namely Henry II, who granted the fortification to the Norman de Camville family. It was this family which is credited with the refortification at Llansteffan, holding possession there until 1338, and reconstructing in two definite phases much of what we see today.

The Welsh continued to target the castle however, capturing and burning it in 1215 and again in 1257.

In 1338 when the de Camville male line died out, Robert de Penres took control, to accompany his other two castles at Penrice and Oxwich. However, de Penres fell from favour with the then King Edward III, having the castle taken off him, and then subsequently convicted on 'suspect' charges of murder.

His son regained the castle by paying off the imposed fine, restoring pride to the family, after Richard II had had temporary custody of Llansteffan; Richard being executed with many of the king's advisors in 1388, before the de Penres name was reinstalled.

Owain Glyndwr is believed to have had brief residence at the castle, but he too lost it back to another member of the de Penres family, Sir John, who wrestled it from Glyndwr in 1403. The castle was then to go back into the hands of the Welsh, only for Sir John to regain it in 1408.

After de Penres died, the castle then went to Henry, Prince of Wales, then subsequently to his brother, the Duke of Gloucester.

Various noblemen then had residence before the Duke of Bedford, Jasper Tudor, had ownership, carrying out some alterations including the blocking of the entrance to the great gatehouse.

The castle then went into near ruin, with even farm buildings being documented as standing all along the curtain walls until when in 1959, the government took over and carried out major restoration.

Today, Llansteffan Castle is under the care of CADW, and open at all reasonable times with no charge for entry.

Find Llanstephan situated on the headland, 7 miles off the B4312, heading south-south-west of Carmarthen. Car Park with uphill walk to castle.

LOUGHOR CASTLE AND SWANSEA CASTLE

One of the most intriguing aspects of castles, is the fact that in this modern world of ours, suddenly, just off a busy road or near a crowded street, you can suddenly find solace in rediscovering a castle, an often overlooked treasure in this 'not a minute to lose' world.

Two such castles that fit into such a category are Loughor Castle and Swansea Castle. Their position often means that they sadly go unnoticed, as people go about their everyday business, which is quite sad really, as both have a lot to offer in terms of history and architecture.

With everything that is going on around you, I've devised a method of transporting yourself back to the time of when the castle was in full use.

In your mind's eye, strip away all that is around the site of the castle, disregarding the new buildings, the traffic on the roads and all the other sights that make up today.

Then, do your best to blot out the noise from the present, and slowly but surely, you'll be left with just the castle, standing with magnificent views all around it in a quite field, or near a river.

Using this technique, you will begin to see that right before your eyes, history being brought to life. Just add in a few cattle, a blue sky backdrop and a few folk going about their daily tasks, and the picture is complete.

Loughor Castle is one such castle where you will need to blot out the heavy traffic, as it now sits alongside the busy A484, on the western edge of Swansea city, near a bridge.

The Normans took advantage of the natural mound positioned here, located at the best point where the Loughor river can be crossed. The castle would have served as a fortified watchtower, overseeing all crossings at this point.

However, invaders prior to the Normans also saw its potential, for it was the Roman soldiers from the Second Augustan Legion who established their fort here in around AD 75, also with the same purpose, to guard this crossing point on the Loughor.

The earthen 'ringwork' of the Norman Castle was thrown up over the south-east turret, the highest point, of this Roman Fort of Leucarum, (Loughor).

This auxiliary fort at Loughor, (or Leucara

in Latin), was probably another link in the chain of many forts that spanned the length of the road that ran from Viroconium, (Wroxeter), to Moridunum, (Carmarthen).

However, by the middle of the 2nd century AD, the Romans had abandoned it, only to temporarily return during the late 3rd and 4th centuries, before they left it for good.

By the 12th century the Normans were busy extending their grip over southern Wales, with Henry de Beaumont becoming the area's overlord.

By 1116, an oval ringwork now existed where once an earlier fort stood, and Henry de Viliers was to be appointed as its first commander.

In 1151, the castle which was then defended with timber ramparts and protecting inner wooden buildings, was attacked and burnt by the Welsh. With a possible link to this event, scorched chess pieces have been unearthed at the site.

Upon regaining Loughor Castle, the Normans set about reconstructing it, making significant repairs and incorporating several stone buildings. Yet again however, in 1215, the castle was once again attacked and badly damaged.

In the early part of the 13th century, the castle was given to John de Braose, the son-in-law of Llywelyn ab Iorwerth. He was to rebuild and add a curtain wall, of which today, only the foundations remain.

By the end of the century William de Braose, synonymous with events at

Abergavenny Castle, had the lordship, and under his direction, the rectangular stone tower that now dominates what it is left of the site, was constructed.

The fireplaces, windows and latrine chute, all point to the tower having been used as a place of residence.

After this period of time, little else is known about Loughor Castle, and in its present form, it now rests under the wing of CADW.

For any visitor to Loughor Castle, , the site is freely accessible at all reasonable times.

Back in the heart of Swansea itself, situated on Castle Street, opposite Castle Gardens, is the city's 14th-century fortress, Swansea Castle.

Also under CADW's wing, views can only be had from outside, but nevertheless, the 'new castle' still stands erect and prominent amongst its neighbouring modern constructions.

We refer to the 'new castle' as opposed to the 'old castle' for the simple reason that when Henry Beaumont, earl of Warwick, captured the Gower in 1099, he built the first Swansea Castle. However, this first earth-and-timber motte and bailey has been completely incorporated into the 'new castle', dating from the early 14th century, classed as a fortified manor house and built by Henry de Gower, Bishop of St, David's.

Before it was incorporated though, records show that the 'old castle' itself was badly damaged in 1115-16, and it is thought that there were no repairs carried out, probably because it was in too much of a state to even contemplate work.

However, de Gower's 'new castle' was to also suffer, this time at the hands of Owain Glyndwr at the beginning of the 15th century, as the rebellion he led swept across Wales.

As we see the 'new castle' at Swansea today, the existing block lay at the southern end of a much larger stronghold construction.

The remains include a hall, solar and service rooms on the first floor, with a series of vaulted basements below.

As to who actually built the most prominent feature at Swansea Castle remains to be seen. Opinion is divided over the building of the magnificent arcaded parapet around the upper walls.

Some suggest it was Henry de Gower's work, as there are similar instances of his handiwork at his palaces in Lamphey and St. David's. Others believe it to be the work of the de Mowbray lord of Gower, who used the bishop's own masons.

In the late 18th century the northern block was remodelled as a debtors' prison, the conditions of which became a Victorian scandal.

Positioned near the city centre, the castle can be seen from surrounding areas only.

M

MANORBIER CASTLE

Situated some 5 miles east of Pembroke stands Manorbier Castle, a truly enchanting fortress that commands views across a peaceful bay, across to Trewent Point, and onto Stackpole Head.

Many castles situated across Wales reflect the times past in which they stood, battle scarred and subsequently ruinous.

In my opinion any ruinous appearance doesn't detract from the character or the beauty of a castle at all, but it has to be said, when you do come across a castle virtually untouched by the ravages of time, you definitely feel closer to the era in which it was built.

This is the case with Manorbier Castle, having only seen two minor skirmishes, the first an assault in 1327, when Richard de Barri put siege to the castle claiming it to be his, and then during the Civil War in 1645, when Oliver Cromwell's Roundheads seized Manorbier and slighted it. From that point onwards, only the elements have left any impression.

Manorbier is of course the birthplace of Giraldus Cambrensis, Gerald of Wales, who was born at the castle in 1146. A major figure in Welsh history, Gerald, a prolific writer, traveller, topographer and churchman, described Manorbier as "the most delightful part Pembroch…the pleasantest spot in Wales". His birthplace, a notably well preserved fortification, stands on a rise overlooking the bay.

Gerald was born son of Norman Lord William de Barri, and Angharad, daughter of the Norman Gerald of Windsor, who at the time had the nearby castle of Carew in his ownership.

Of Manorbier, Gerald wrote further, "the castle…is excellently well defended by turrets and bulwarks, and is situated on the summit of a hill…having on the northern and southern sides a fine fish pond under its walls as conspicuous for its grand appearance as for the depths of its waters…and a beautiful orchard on the same side".

It is also interesting to note that apart from the fishponds there was a vineyard, which would account for his incorporation of the word 'orchard', reflecting a more warmer climate during the time.

Gerald of Wales was also regarded as passionately Welsh, commanding wide respect for his beliefs and intellect, and whilst recruiting for the Third Crusade along with Archbishop Baldwin, he became famous for his "Itinerary of Wales".

Manorbier Castle was constructed in the 12th Century by the de Barri family, replacing an earlier wooden structure on the site. Many additions were made by John be Barri, spanning a period of some 50 years, following work carried out earlier at the beginning of the 12th Century by Lord de Barri.

Research indicates that any early motte and bailey set-up was probably attributable to Odo de Barri, William de Barri's father and Gerald's grandfather.

Lord Barri, (who gave his name to the coastal town of Barry, the now popular seaside resort), started work on Manorbier during the reign of Henry I, and the earlier construction of a hall, a small tower beside the square gatehouse remains today.

Two more pieces to the equation as to why Manorbier Castle looks so 'fresh' so to speak, is the durability of the local limestone from which it was built, and the efforts of one J.R. Cobb, who being an antiquarian and castle lover, was responsible for not just Manorbier's restoration, but other castles in Pembrokeshire too.

Cobb leaves behind restored floors, both in the tower and gatehouse, plus new windows and repairs to stonework, the legacy of someone who gave their heart to keeping a part of Welsh history alive, for future generations to enjoy and savour.

Once described by an historian as a "most perfect model of an old Norman baron's residence, with all its appendages, church, mill, dove house, ponds, park and grove", Manorbier Castle really is a fusion of many attributes, one of comfort, function and fortification.

The outer bailey comprises the not unusual format of earthen embankments and ditches, reinforced by stone, with the rectangular

gatehouse making for a lovely beckoning backdrop.

The gatehouse itself incorporates strong battlements, portcullis and arrow-slits, so any invader who had made slowed progress over the outer bailey, would be further greeted by bowmen's arrows.

The gatehouse also comprised machicolations, so if the invader were to progress into the passageway of the gatehouse, narrow openings within the passageway would of allowed any intruder to have been pelted with whatever came to hand, be it solid missiles or liquids of a potent and perhaps boiling nature.

The inner ward consists of a strong curtainwall with corner towers, a complex hall range and large barn, with the most fascinating feature of all being the massive industrial hearths on the west and southern walls. Also built into the curtain wall was a hall-keep, built into the wall as opposed to standing as a structure by itself, as in many other castles.

The centre of all activity revolved around the great hall built in the 1140's, with service buildings built adjacent to it. These included the buttery, pantry, kitchens and ovens. It is above the buttery in the original drawing room of William de Barri, that Gerald is most likely to have been born.

A further claim to fame is that the great hall is possibly the earliest surviving stone building at any castle in west Wales.

On the southern side of the great hall, the chapel, spur tower and watergate were housed. The spur tower containing the latrines and the watergate allowing access the bay. All these attributes plus the elaborate inner decor seen throughout Manorbier, indicates the status the de Barri family had, maintaining control of the castle up until 1359, when after several ownership changes, it became the property of the monarchy in the late 15th Century.

By 1630, Queen Elizabeth had sold the castle to the Bowen's of Trefloyne, and by 1670 it had changed hands again, this time to the Phillippses of Picton Castle. It wasn't until the late 19th century that it was eventually in the care of J.R. Cobb.

Today Manorbier is in private ownership, and to the best of my knowledge in the hands of Lady Dunsany, a Phillips descendant.

It is located in stunning scenery off the A4139 and then along the narrow country lane, the B4585.

The Castle is open daily to the public, Easter until September, 10.30 a.m., until 5.30 p.m. For further details contact *(01834) 871394.*

MONMOUTH CASTLE

Situated between Abergavenny and Ross-on-Wye is the market town of Monmouth, birthplace in 1387 of the future King Henry V and home to a battle torn castle built to command crossings of the Wye and Monnow rivers.

The castle was originally established by William FitzOsbern of Breteuil, Earl of Hereford and one of William the Conqueror's most trusted barons.

The first castle at Monmouth was built during the period 1067 to 1071, and was of a chain of strongholds erected to defend his territory and ultimately 'hold' south-east Wales. With the protection of the castle in place along with a Benedictine priory, Monmouth grew into a Norman settlement. The town was listed in the Domesday Book of 1086 as part of Herefordshire.

By 1100, Monmouth had become an important place and had all but completely broken away from Herefordshire, becoming the seat of the Marcher Lordship of Monmouth, William FitzBaderon.

Monmouth Castle and surrounding estates would remain in his family name until 1256, having in the meantime during their occupation, constructed the Great Tower, (or Norman Hall).

When the last of male line of the family died, the castle was granted to Prince Edward, son of Henry III, who was to become King Edward I, and to this day, has become known as the most capable and most ruthless king ever to sit on the English throne.

During the time under the control of Edward, the castle was captured by Simon de Montfort, leader of the English barons who had an understanding with Llewelyn ap Gruffudd, the first Welsh-born prince ever to use the title 'Prince of Wales', Llewelyn having a great mistrust of Edward.

Prince Edward regained the castle when he commanded the army which defeated Simon's forces, which included many Welsh archers, at Kenilworth.

In 1267, Edward granted Monmouth Castle, along with Grosmont Skenfrith and White Castle, (better known as 'The Three Castles'), to his younger brother, Edmund 'Crouchback', upon him being bestowed Earl of Lancaster.

It was under the ownership of the Earl, that the Great Hall, a large rectangular building, was added on the south side of the Great Tower. The Hall was a single storey building, containing one large room used for the holding of courts. It functioned as a courtroom right up until the 17th century.

In September 1387, the Great Tower bore witness to a royal birth, that of future King Henry V. Henry, victor of Agincourt and Shakespeare's 'Harry Monmouth', was the son of the Duke of Lancaster, who had himself become Henry IV, following the forced abdication of Richard II in 1399. Richard was son of the Black Prince, both of whom had large and loyal bodies of Welsh supporters.

It is during the 14th century the Great Tower went through transformation with the insertion of large decorated windows. The old entrance was replaced and a tall door inserted whilst the Tower roof was being renewed.

With Richard II imprisoned at Pontefract and Henry's seizure of the throne, Owain Glyndwr, was to take centre stage in an attempt to unite Wales under its own ruler.

Glyndwr, the last Welshman to hold the title of Prince of Wales, was striving to rid Wales of outside interference and give the Welsh their independence back once and for all, thus instilling the ideal of self rule.

There was growing unease throughout Wales, and the new and extremely unpopular King Henry VI, was seen as the enemy to be faced up to and beaten.

The rebellion against Henry was sparked off by yet another land dispute, of which there were many at this time. One of the King's cronies, Lord Grey of Ruthin, was at loggerheads with a middle-aged country gentleman of great respectability, over a piece of land Lord Grey had 'acquired'. That gentleman was Owain Glyndwr, and this was to be the catalyst for the start of hostilities.

Owain although fighting a stand for the Welsh, was although thought to be fighting too for Richard II, holding out until he was to return and be rightfully reinstated as King. The Welsh had felt more comfortable under the reign of Richard II, indeed showing loyalty to the crown, but alas Richard was not to return and in fact was never seen again.

Owain gathered his supporters, and using the estates in north-east Wales as a base, prepared for battle.

Many a battle was to ensue, including ultimate revenge against Lord Grey, who was taken prisoner at the Battle of Bryn Glas in the summer of 1402, where two thousand of Henry's men fell.

After a defeat at Grosmont Castle, Owain retaliated in 1404 by massacring an English force at Craig y Dorth near Monmouth.

By 1406, Owain was more or less in control of Wales, but even though that seemed to be the battle for his Welsh kingdom won, it wasn't to last and with the personal tragedy of having his wife, daughter and four grandchildren taken prisoner at Harlech Castle in 1409, it all seemed to be falling apart. Allies were murdered and losses on the battlefields were taking their toll and despite being offered a pardon in 1412, he lived out the remainder of his life as a fugitive with his death recorded in 1416.

Monmouth Castle's defences were not put to the test again until the Civil War of 1642. The castle changed hands three times between the Parliamentarians and the Royalists and when under Parliamentarian control, and the leadership of one Colonel Massey, had fought many battles with the Royalists at nearby Raglan Castle.

With the fall of Monmouth and its Castle in 1645 and then later Raglan Castle, total control of South Wales and the Marches went to theParliamentarians.

In the Spring of 1647, an order was given to slight the Monmouth Castle. The Great Tower fell of its own accord months later, thought to have been weakened not just by the order to slight it, but by tunnelling under the Tower made by Parliamentarians in an attempt to sabotage it when in their hands.

The Castle then passed into the possession of Henry Somerset who built the Great Castle House in 1673, replacing Raglan as his family's residence following the Civil War.

In 1801, the House became a girls' school and in 1875 headquarters of the Royal Monmouthshire Royal Engineers and as such, still remains one of the few British castles still in military occupation.

OGMORE CASTLE

Situated just 2 miles to the south west of Bridgend stands Ogmore Castle. Along with neighbouring castles at Newcastle and Coity, these three formed the defence of the western boundary of Glamorgan in Norman times.

Early constructions on the site of Ogmore Castle, suggest an earth and timber type structure which took the form of a 'ringwork', encompassed by a series of ditches. It was most likely constructed by William de Londres, ('of London'). Londres was known to be in the area before 1116 when most journals point to the building work being started.

We also know that it was William's son, Maurice, who is responsible for the construction of Ewenny Priory, 2 miles to the south of Bridgend. This was considered to be a further fortified position to hold the western boundary, along with the three castles. The priory was founded in 1411 as a cell of the Benedictine abbey of Gloucester, which is of course now a Cathedral. The priory still houses Maurice's tomb.

Ogmore Castle was built with a multi purpose in mind, Firstly, to guard the stepping stones across the small Ewenny river and to also guard the ford across the larger Ogmore at nearby Merthyr Mawr.

Not long after the original structure was built, Ogmore was to rather quickly acquire an impressive and powerful stone keep. This was probably built by Maurice and was one of the earliest 12th Century stone keeps in Wales. The west wall of the keep is still standing today to a proud height of 40 feet, the other walls however have fallen away somewhat.

The keep, which is a rectangular tower some three stories high, was made from huge boulders, set together in mortar.

On the first floor of the keep, there is evidence of a hall. The interior of the ground floor, would have only been reached through passing through a trapdoor from the first, a defensive design which was quite commonplace and indeed, the normal pattern to find in these type of structures. The first floor also boasts two round-headed windows and a also a rare find for this period in history, a fireplace.

A third storey was to be added at a later date, with the tower having its roof raised to accommodate it. This was to be the private apartment of the resident lord, but the original line of where the roof was can still be seen, marked by a line of guttering lower down.

To the north of the Bridgend town centre today, Newcastle, the other important stronghold stands. The ruins of this castle are dated to the second half of the 12th Century, although documentation points towards there

being a structure there around 1106. There is however, a great deal of speculation concerning many aspects of the castle's building, re-siting etc.

With Ogmore Castle now in the possession of Maurice de Londres, now elevated to Baron status, he was to fight alongside the Lord of Kidwelly, in the battle of Maes Gwenllian of 1136.

The Welsh, now uniting against the invaders following Henry I's death, were led by Gwenllian, wife of Gryffydd ap Rhys of Deheubarth.

Gwenllian had stepped into the breach of matters, when she had heard news that reinforcements for Maurice de Londres' forces had landed on the coast of Glamorgan.

With her husband away asking for assistance from his father-in-law, Gruffudd ap Cynan, Lord of North Wales, she decided to intercept the force before it arrived at its destination of Kidwelly Castle.

With her two sons at her side, Maelgwn and Morgan, the heroic Princess rode out to make sure they were stopped.

Unfortunately, things did not go to plan. Rather than stay as one unit, she had divided her forces, sending one detachment to engage Maurice's reinforcements, whilst keeping the remainder of her army back, hidden some two miles from Kidwelly Castle.

The approaching Norman army however, under the command of Welsh traitor Gruffudd ap LLewellyn, had other plans. They had taken a different roundabout route, evading the men sent to cut them off and instead, ambushed Gwenllian's remaining forces near the castle.

At this moment, Maurice himself entered the fray with an army from within Kidwelly Castle and a slaughter ensued of Gwenllian's troops. With her one son Maelgwn killed at her side trying to protect her, the fight was soon over and with the remainder of he men, Gwenllian was taken prisoner and summarily executed on the spot, her head being hacked from her body as her other son Morgan watched in horror.

Gwenllian, for her gallantry and courage, will always be remembered and celebrated in Welsh folk history as 'The gallant Gwenllian who battle till death'. Hence the name of the battle and its site, Maes Gwenllian, "maes" being Welsh for "field of".

When Roger, the Bishop of Salisbury died, Maurice de Londres gained Kidwelly Castle, which the Bishop had built in 12th Century. From then on the fortunes of Kidwelly and Ogmore Castle were tied up with the de Londres family.

In the early 13th Century, more work was to be carried out at Ogmore Castle. Firstly a rather weak stone curtain wall was added on top of the line of timber defences. This guarded the newly built domestic buildings in the inner ward. With a moat on three sides of the castle and the Ewenny river on the north side, a gateway was constructed next to the keep and this would have incorporated a drawbridge at the front during its time. Other improvements included a turret on the other side of the keep, housing two sets of latrines. Along with a new hall standing at the north

end of the inner ward, a lime kiln was to be added to the outer ward.

In the later part of the 13th century, Ogmore passed on to the Chaworths of Kidwelly, and subsequently through marriages to the earls, later dukes, of Lancaster.

From then on, the castle was used as a prison, and then as a centre of administration and justice for its lordship. The castle and the stepping stones across the river, were then placed in the ownership of the Government of the Duchy of Lancaster in 1928.

OXWICH CASTLE AND PENRICE CASTLE

Situated 11 miles to the south-west of Swansea on the Gower Peninsula lies Penrice Castle, ancestral home of the de Penres family with connections at neighbouring Oxwich Castle to the west of it, and Llanstephan Castle to the north.

Penrice itself was on a foreland site, and the beginnings of the structure we see today were built as the successor to an earthwork fortification of nearby Mounty Brough, erected not far from a church.

About the time of his marriage in 1237, Robert de Penres transferred building to the other side of the ravine, north of the church, and set about constructing a round keep, and a thin curtain wall which ran north east.

The keep comprised a single room with three windows plus a latrine, but no fireplace. It was later to be raised giving no extra living space, but overall providing a unique single storey chemise incorporating a flat roof and parapet.

Following the Welsh revolt during the 1260's, de Penres went on to enclose the rest of the site with stone walls, together with tiny round flanking turrets.

A barn was added on the north east side and on the west side which was deemed more vulnerable, redevelopment took place, adding a hall and gatehouse.

Today, Penrice Castle stands as the largest castle on the Gower and the ivy clad ruins show a keep; a double towered gatehouse; two round towers and five small turrets. The curtain walls vary somewhat in thickness whilst the keep walls have been measured at over two metres thick.

A later Robert de Penres, who married into the powerful Camville family, incurred the wrath of Edward III in 1367, for allowing the castle to fall into disrepair, claiming the safety of the realm had been endangered by him allowing it to do so.

His estates including Penrice were subsequently forfeited in 1377, when under suspect circumstances, de Penres was convicted of the murder of a woman at Llanstephan, which he had allegedly committed seven years earlier.

The castle was regained by his son, another Robert de Penres, who bought back the estates in 1391 but with no heirs to leave everything too, they were passed onto the Mansels of Oxwich.

Sir Rice Mansel then later let the castle to William Benet, who heirs resided at the castle until 1669.

It is thought that the defences at Penrice Castle were dismantled in the Civil War, with a branch of the Mansel family using it as tenanted farm during the 18th Century.

Penrice Castle now stands on private land, but there is a public footpath giving you right of way, allowing viewing of portions of the curtain and towers.

Oxwich Castle is situated not far away, standing on headland which forms the west side of Oxwich bay, one of the Gower Peninsula's most popular south coast beaches. With some three miles of sand backed up by a high barrier of dunes, coupled with woods along the headland leading to Oxwich Point, most of this area is within a National Nature Reserve.

The castle in reality, is a magnificent Tudor mansion with mock-military embellishments created by the vision of Sir Rice Mansel, although the mansion's history does point towards an earlier true stronghold on the site.

The early castle at Oxwich belonged to the de Penres family, with Robert de Penres taking Penrice Castle for himself, and leaving Oxwich Castle for the rest of his family. All this upon his marriage into the far more noble de Camville family, his then wife being heiress to Llanstephan Castle.

It is however the Mansel family to which we attribute the construction of today, a testimony to the years of the 16th century and built during peaceful and prosperous times by one of number of minor gentry families in South Wales, who had gained power, prestige and property under the reign of Tudor monarchs.

Another example of this lifestyle which mirrored that of earlier feudal magnates in appearance, is that of Beaupre Castle, near Cowbridge in South Glamorgan.

Beaupre, meaning 'Beautiful Retreat', the castle incorporates a remarkable inner porch, probably the finest of its kind in Wales. The porch's architect being Sir Richard Bassett of the Bassett family of long standing residence. With a central shield carrying Sir Richard's arms above the doorway and lavish decorative carvings, this really is a glorious piece of architecture.

Sir Rice Mansel also had his coat of arms emblazoned on the gateway he constructed at Oxwich Castle, which upon passing through, entered into an enclosed courtyard. The courtyard having two adjacent ranges of buildings, both of which appear to have been designed independently and could well of functioned as households in their own right.

Sir Rice Mansel, (1487-1559), was a veteran of the wars in Ireland and between 1542 and 1546, had served in the wars against France and Scotland. He had also had the status of Chamberlain of Chester and was a member of the Council of the Marches, with Queen Mary appointing him as chamberlain and chancellor of South Wales.

The history books indicate that this south-ern-range and gateway were the work of Sir Rice Mansel in around 1520 to 1538, with the east range designed and constructed as a singular vision by his son, Sir Edward, around 1559 to 1580.

Sir Edward Mansel's eastern range is of complex and elegant design, with a first floor hall and impressive long gallery above. The surviving six storey tower-like block, represents one of three projections on the eastern side, all of these vast and grandiose. This was the accommodation for the Mansel family, together with a multitude of retainers.

By 1632, Oxwich Castle had been leased as a residence and whilst the east range fell into disrepair, the south range continued to function as a farmhouse.

Lady Aspley is responsible for stepping in to save Oxwich from demolition in 1949, having the castle placed in state care and today after a considerable program of conservation and reconstruction, it rests in CADW's hands as a Welsh historical monument.

Oxwich Castle is open to the public. For dates and times telephone *(01792) 390359* for information.

P

PENHOW CASTLE

Penhow Castle boldly states the claim that it is Wales' oldest inhabited castle, and with the Welsh nation having more castles per square mile than anywhere else in Europe, it's quite a boast. All the research though does support this claim, making Penhow quite a jewel in county of Monmouthshire's crown.

Penhow Castle is situated just off the A48 road, some 7 miles east of Newport. Access to the castle itself is easy, but seeing as it is still in private ownership, you will need to ring ahead to negotiate a convenient visiting time, (telephone number at the end of the article).

Penhow is a perfect example of the smaller type of fortified manor house and was developed from an initially built keep, constructed to protect the knightly retainers of the local earl, who resided at Chepstow Castle.

These "Knight's Fee" manors were established to protect farmland and areas surrounding Chepstow Castle, serving as a sort of 'look-out post' for any trouble, which duly came from the Welsh.

Chepstow has a truly fine castle; situated high above the River Wye to the north end of the town, the fortress stands as a mighty and impressive guardian overlooking one of the main crossing points from southern England into Wales.

Families were settling into the area known then as Gwent, (now as Monmouthshire), when William the Conqueror invaded. In 1129, the ownership of Penhow came into the hands of Sir Roger de St Maur.

In return for keeping the feisty Welsh at bay, Sir Roger was allowed to usurp the Manor of Penhow from its native Welsh prince, and thus gain a foot of the feudal ladder.

Other tasks bestowed upon him included providing a quota of men for guard duty at Chepstow Castle every month and to a lesser extent, providing one solitary man on horseback in times of war.

By the mid 13th Century, the great marcher lordship of Chepstow, under which Penhow fell, was in the hands of the powerful Marshal family. This family were also the earls of Pembroke and Sir William de St. Maur of Penhow was to marry the 3rd daughter of the earl.

William Marshall was famous as an outstanding soldier of fortune, and using his vast knowledge of military architecture, had set about bringing his newly inherited Chepstow Castle up to date.

Henry III is chronicled to have stayed at the Chepstow Castle in the summer of 1217, two years before the death of Marshall in 1219.

Having married this third daughter, it could only mean that links were strengthened for

Sir William not just by the ownership of one of the properties governed under the lordship of Chepstow, but by now being part of an extremely wealthy and powerful family.

Indeed, a agreement was entered into by Sir William and his brother-in-law Gilbert Marshal, to deprive the last prince of Gwent, Morgan ap Howell, of his manor at 'Woundy', now known as Undy, which was situated 4 miles from Penhow Castle. The agreement meant that between them, Sir William and Gilbert could carve up the disputed land between them which included vineyards.

It also meant that were any attempts made to take Woundy, then Sir William could call upon the formidable army of his brother-in-law, to crush any opposition.

By the end of the 14th Century and with some of the family now moving away from Penhow, the fortress now found itself without a male heir and the then resident Isabella Seymour was to marry John Bowles, adopting the arms of the Seymour family.

In 1430 John Bowles died, and from there it was his grandson Thomas Bowles, who was to make Penhow stand out in history again, by undertaking the extraordinary endeavour of leading a small force of men from Gwent, all the way to the Scottish border to assist in the siege of Berwick-upon-Tweed.

For his services in this battle, which was a splinter element of the War of the Roses, Thomas was knighted by the Duke of Gloucester, subsequently returning home with a healthy pension.

Thomas was then to marry Sir Thomas Morgan's daughter Maud and his family's coat of arms, the simple paired wings of the hunting lure, were incorporated into that of the Morgan family, a griffin or dragon.

This combined arms is carved in stone on the outside of one the windows of the great hall at Penhow.

In 1674, Thomas Lewis of St. Pierre bought Penhow Castle, and from this point onwards and during the Civil War, documentation about the castle becomes sketchy to say the least, although it does seem that it survived as liveable habitation throughout this time.

By 1714, it is known that Penhow was owned by absent landlords and was tenanted as a farm.

By 1973, the film director and writer Stephen Weeks bought the castle, carrying out substantial restoration work on the property, enough so to allow visitors to view the site.

As far as construction goes, Penhow is essentially made up of three successive houses arranged around a central courtyard, these being a medieval keep; a 15th Century hall block and a late Stuart house.

The main buildings on view to the public are the 12th Century keep towers including its ramparts; the 13th Century curtain wall; the lower hall of the 14th and 15th Century; the dovecot, and the Tudor wing.

The lower hall, now the entrance to the castle, was probably used as a retainer's hall in the time of the residence of Sir Thomas Bowles, and adjoining that was the tiny Porter's Room.

For any visitor to the area who has the day to browse, it is also worth considering a tour of other castles in the area. Three particular such sights immediately spring to mind, that of Raglan Castle; Caldicot Castle and Chepstow Castle, all within comfortable distances of Penhow.

At the time of writing, Penhow Castle is up for sale, which is why either visiting the Penhow Castle official website, or calling *(01633) 400800* is imperative before visiting.

Situated est off Newport, just off the A48. No parking charges. Head of M4 at junction 24 towards Penhow along the A48.

PENNARD CASTLE AND OYSTERMOUTH CASTLE

It's difficult not to romanticise about castles situated on the coastline. Views of the rugged cliffs with the sea below, conjure up all sorts of images of how a castle, occupied and lit-up at night, may have looked to any approaching visitor.

That is just the sort of vision one may have on approaching Pennard Castle, sited 1/2 mile south of the village of Parkmill on the A4118, 8 miles south-west of the city of Swansea.

Access to the castle is via a coastal footpath against the backdrop of the the Three Cliffs Bay, which Pennard Castle overlooks along with the view across the valley to Penmaen Burrows.

The now majestic ruin is perched high on the edge of the valley of Pennard Pill, a steep drop below it to the north and west.

In the 12th century Henry de Beaumont, first earl of Warwick, was granted lordship of the Gower, and it is thought that it was probably he who built the initial ringwork castle. This incorporated a bank and ditch around it, and a primitive stone hall.

In the 13th century, under the ownership of the de Braose's, the castle was rebuilt in stone, using local limestone and reddish sandstone. In 1321, Pennard Castle then changed hands, passing into the Mowbray family.

Time and weather have left its mark on the castle, and although during the period of its construction it was thought to have been built on a near perfect site, the builders didn't realise that the castle was vulnerable to 'sand blow', and the eventual encroachment of the sand was to in fact lead to the castle's abandonment by the end of the 14th century.

It is interesting to note that on the opposite side of the valley at Penmaen, there was a similar castle erected at around the same time. This however is a complete ruin, with only traces left of this castle, including the lower part of the hall at the west end of its courtyard.

Sand now covers the courtyard at Pennard Castle, and on the windward side, the greater part of the curtain wall has collapsed, although, some repairs have been undertaken since 1961.

The twin-towered gatehouse is the most impressive feature at Pennard, with the best views of the castle being gained when looking at it from the north, where the curtain wall is almost intact.

The hall would of incorporated a private room for the resident lord, twin service rooms and a principal room, which would of had a roaring fire in the hearth.

A small settlement grew up around the castle, and to its east, a solitary section of wall is all that's left of St. Mary's church, which along with the castle and indeed the village that once was, has all been overwhelmed by the sand.

Judging by its over all construction, the castle is small and rather crudely built. Throughout the fortress, there seems to be little understanding of military architecture by the builders, this theory being supported by two square holes of unknown purpose from the guardsroom to the passage, and the ineffective arrow slits.

Apart from Pennard Castle which stands on the edge of the golf links, Parkmill also has another place of interest. To the north-west of the village is a hidden valley that has been inhabited by man since prehistoric times. Stone Age inhabitants built Parc le Breos, a stone burial chamber dating back some 6000 years, whose foundations can still be seen.

A little further up the valley is an even older site, Cathole Cave, containing bones of a mammoth and woolly rhinoceros. The cave was inhabited towards the end of the Ice Age, some 10,000 years ago.

Travelling 4 miles south-west of Swansea and off the A4067, you eventually arrive at Swansea Bay on the Mumbles.

The Mumbles is a popular resort in itself, preserving something of a Victorian feel to it. The rocks and the lighthouse at Mumbles Head, mark the start of the Gower Peninsula, and elevated above all this in a grassy setting, stands Oystermouth Castle, which unlike Pennard Castle, is exceptionally preserved. The name Oystermouth deriving from a Norman/English corruption of Ystmllwynarth.

For views across Swansea Bay, Mumbles Pier provides ample vantage with the bays of Bracelet and Limeslade close by.

The first stronghold on this site was probably built by Henry Beaumont, Earl of Warwick, before the end of the 11th century. This followed Beaumont being made Lord of Gower by Henry I.

The Welsh had destroyed anything that had existed on the site before in 1287, during a violent uprising of that year. It was the de Braose family who rebuilt the fortress as it stands today in the 13th century. Edward I having stayed at the castle for two days in 1284.

When it was reconstructed, Oystermouth Castle was rebuilt as a courtyard castle. At the one end was an impressive three-storey gatehouse, the top floor of which being occupied by a chapel. A traceried window can still be seen, along with a stone basin used in the rinsing of the chalice during services.

The gatehouse did once have two round towers, Oliver Cromwell being blamed for their destruction, although I can find no history of the castle being involved in the Civil War.

This non-involvement however, would account for the exceptional state of preservation at Oystermouth Castle, so much so, that the fortress still stands to its original height.

The grooves for the wheels taking the chains of the drawbridge can still be seen, and whilst the original portcullis is no more, a copy of it now stands in the entrance. Having entered, a flight of stone steps to the left beside the guardroom leads to the eloquently entitled 'White Lady's Chamber', one of the governor's principal apartments.

The keep is notable for its gracious apartments and stunning windows, of which the work of those in the banqueting hall, reflects an early English style.

Remodelling at the castle went on into the 16th century and its easy to see why Oystermouth Castle would of made such a desirable residence during its time.

Pennard Castle can be viewed all year round, whilst for information on visiting times at Oystermouth Castle, telephone *(01792) 635444* for details.

R

RAGLAN CASTLE

Situated between Monmouth and Abergavenny just of the A40 in south east Wales, is the village of Raglan. On higher ground overlooking the village stands its magnificent sprawling castle which, quite possibly, was the last great castle to be built at the end of the Middle Ages.

Historians remain somewhat divided about the castle and when the initial structure was built, (not the one which stands there today). There is however strong evidence to suggest that there was such a fortification on the site as far back as the mid-12th Century. This is supported by the fact that the castle is on a motte and bailey site, which could only have dated from that era.

Other historians say it dates back to the days of Sir William Thomas, who fought with Henry V at Agincourt in 1415. The Castle has also been linked with Sir John Morley, and the belief that he was Lord of Raglan Castle in 1377.

Whatever is thought of its early construction, it is more than likely that the current construction, was probably built with the Wars of Roses in mind.

We know that the Welsh were greatly involved on both sides of the Wars of the Roses, the eastern side of Wales strongly supporting York because of the influences of the Mortimer family who owned large estates on the Marches, other parts of Wales being more divided.

William Herbert, Earl of Pembroke, is credited with what we see of the Castle today. The work here starting in 1430 and going on until 1470 as the Earl set about remodelling the Castle in the contemporary French style of the time.

Raglan Castle was considered by writers of the time to be a magnificent stronghold, boasting an impressive hexagonal keep, 'Melin y Gwent', (Yellow Tower of Gwent), with walls ten feet thick. The keep, surrounded by its own chemise wall, was based on the latest military thinking of that time, proving a foreboding sight to would-be invaders.

The keep, which was five storeys high, was separated from the rest of castle by a moat and a double drawbridge. Further defensives included three large and two small multi angular towers.

As a professional soldier, William Herbert had been a staunch Yorkist, having fought with the armies of Henry VI. It was his support for Edward IV at Mortimer's Cross that earned him the title of Baron Herbert.

He was created Knight of the Garter in 1462 before becoming Earl of Pembroke in 1468 as a reward for taking Harlech Castle. He was to be made Earl however just before his death in 1469, when he was captured by the Lancastrians at the Battle of Banbury and beheaded. Over 2,000 Welshmen perished with him, either on the battlefield or later on the chopping block.

With the defeat of Richard III and his forces on the battlefield at Bosworth, Henry VII was installed as King and the Wars of the Roses were to come to an end. Francis Bacon wrote of Henry, "To the Welsh people his victory was theirs; they had thereby regained their liberty".

One thing is clear, when the Wars ended, it heralded the demise of the medieval systems throughout England, and there would have been no such undertaking to build a castle like Raglan Castle again.

It wasn't until 1642 when the Civil War broke out, that Raglan Castle was to once again become prominent.

Opinion in Wales wasn't all one sided when hostilities commenced, but the majority rallied to the call of King Charles I, even though it was generally considered that forces of whatever nature should be halted from crossing the Welsh border. Raglan Castle, upon declaring its support for the King, stamped its authority in Monmouthshire and saw the rest of county follow suit in showing its allegiance.

By now, Raglan Castle was something of a 'show-piece', divided into two courts, the 'Stone' and the 'Fountain'. These in turn, were separated from one another by what was a 60 foot high building, including a magnificent great hall measuring 66 foot by 28 foot, with a rare geometrical roof made from Irish Oak, and lit from a large cupola. The Fountain Court housed the Castle's state apartments.

Along with the great hall was the then Earl's private dining room, a buttery, drawing room, gallery and numerous fountain displays, one of which spouting a column of water as high as the castle walls.

Raglan Castle was frequently visited by Charles I. One notable visit was following his defeat of the New Model Army at Naseby on 14th June 1645, with his arrival at the castle some three weeks in July.

During this time, Raglan Castle was involved in a series of battles with neighbouring Monmouth Castle, which had been captured and was now used as a base by the Parlimentarians. Raglan and its defensives held firm during this time, proving its worth as a skillful piece of modern day military architecture.

History now recalls one Oliver Cromwell, who sought to rid Welsh territory of Loyalist support. Cromwell was thorough in his destruction of Welsh castles, one of which being Aberystwyth Castle which was virtually raised to the ground because of its production of King's silver coinage. Raglan Castle was one of the last to fall in 1646, after a lengthy siege on its defences by Sir Thomas Fairfax.

Following the end of the Civil War, most castles fell into disrepair, or were stripped of their resources for use in the construction of new buildings. Raglan was no exception, with its timber finding its way to Bristol, to help on a bridge reconstruction.

The Castle was restored in 1660, and King Charles II who was then on the throne, made the present Earl of that time, a 2nd Marquess.

The Marquess who was something of an inventer, continued his experiments with water and steam, later writing a scientific paper describing in detail an engine, which upon further development became the first steam driven pump.

Following that period in history, the Castle has once again fallen silent and today makes a wonderful sight against the skyline as you approach from Monmouth. Under CADW, it's open to the public along with an information centre.

Parking is free and just outside the front of the castle. Situated 7 miles south-west of Monmouth off the A40, or 10 miles north-east of Pontypool off the A40. Follow the road from Abergavenny, as if heading towards Monmouth. For further information contact (01291) 690228.

S

SKENFRITH CASTLE AND GROSMONT CASTLE

Skenfrith Castle, together with its neighbouring castle at Grosmont, make up two of the fortresses purposely built to guard routes from England into Wales, and from the threat of the Welsh during medieval times. 'White Castle' makes up the third jigsaw piece, sited near Llantilio Crosenny and not named as the other two are by the village within which it stands, but because of the white plaster rendering which once adorned its walls and towers, traces of which can still be seen today.

Skenfrith Castle was a key border defence fortress and with its sister castles were collectively known as 'The Three Castles', or the 'Monmouthshire Trilateral', controlling a stretch of borderline that was strategically and militarily important at that time.

The castle at Skenfrith can be found by heading out of Abergavenny and picking up the B4521, which incidentally will also bring you to 'White Castle' as well, if you follow the CADW signs. Skenfrith village also has an interesting old church, which along with the castle, stand beside a loop in the in River

Monnow, deep inside virtually undisturbed border country.

The surrounding land is wide and rolling, and it's this gap of land between the cliffs of the Wye valley and the Black Mountains to the north-west, that the three were built to defend. Skenfrith Castle however had the other important roll of keeping a watchful eye over the River Monnow, monitoring any crossings day and night.

The remains of the castle date from the 13th Century, and the round keep on the motte is its principal feature.

In 1201, as a reward for faithful service, King John granted all three castles into the ownership of Hubert de Burgh, an officer in the royal service. Four years later in 1205 he lost possession of them when he became a prisoner of war in France. He was to regain what was rightfully his a number of years later, but in the meantime, the castles fell into the hands of one William de Braose, synonymous with the brutal murders of a group of Welsh chiefs at nearby Abergavenny Castle in 1176, during a so-called 'peace conference'.

By 1219, Hubert de Burgh, now Justiciar of England and earl of Kent, had regained ownership of the 'The Three Castles' and set about modernising Skenfrith Castle. Firstly, he completely levelled the earth and timber castle that had once stood on the site, and replaced it all with an up-to-date stone construction. During his time in France and his warfare with King Philip Augustus, much of what de Burgh was to build seemed to echo French fortress style architecture, with the castle being dominated by the circular keep, standing at the centre of a circular ward, with a round tower at each of the angles. At the time there were probably five towers, but only four remain.

What we see of Skenfrith Castle today is mainly due to the work of Hubert de Burgh, because after he surrendered the castle along with Grosmont and White Castle in 1239 to Henry III, there doesn't seem to have been any significant additions made.

Access to the castle would of been across a bridge crossing the moat to the gatehouse on the north side. The keep was originally entered via a timber staircase at first floor level, whilst above on the second floor, a fireplace gives good indication that this level provided domestic accommodation.

Right at the top of the tower, archers would of taken up position, giving fire from all parts of the castles onto surrounding areas below, a total 360° cover.

The corner towers were used for storage, and access to these would of been via raised doors above ground level, so installed this high for extra security.

In 1936, Skenfrith Castle was given to the National Trust, and guardianship entrusted to the Department of the Environment.

In 2003, CADW accepted responsibility for the protection of the castle from the effects of riverbank erosion. If not challenged the erosion could damage the castle walls.

The village of Grosmont, from the French Gros mont, 'Big Hill', is situated 9 miles north-east of Abergavenny on the B4347. Grosmont also has a rather large church, that

of St. Nicholas, which will strike any visitor as being quite big for such a small community, a consequence of having a castle of such importance and the fact that Grosmont was a borough until 1857.

The earliest construction on the site of the castle was of earth and timber, to be replaced under Hubert de Burgh by the stone fortress, which still looks impressive today.

The main features left to inspect are the ruins of the inner ward gateway, part of the central hall, and two towers on the enclosing wall.

The rectangular two-storey hall block was probably built between 1201 and 1205. The ground floor served as a basement with the main rooms accessed by a timber staircase, situated on the first floor. After his return from France, as with Skenfrith, he turned to modernising Grosmont, adding a stone curtain, with a gatehouse and circular projecting walls at the angles.

In 1233, Henry III was in residence at Grosmont Castle. He had deemed it necessary to visit Grosmont to impose a royal presence and hopefully deter Welsh leader, Llewelyn the Great, who had been causing much unrest in the area, so much so, that even some of the Border Lords loyal to the King, had shown support for Llewelyn.

During a daring night attack however, Henry and his queen were forced to flee into the darkness, as the castle was taken by Llewelyn and his supporters.

Much later Owain Glyndwr held the castle, but in what turned out to be one of his last defeats, lost the castle to Henry of Monmouth, (later Henry V), in 1410.

The 'Three Castles' are situated in relatively close proximity, making it possible to visit all three in one day. Grosmont Castle and Skenfrith Castle respectively, are open to the public all year around at all reasonable hours, whilst White Castle is open from 18th April to 24th September daily between 10 a.m. and 5 p.m. and between October to March at all reasonable hours.

T

TRETOWER CASTLE AND CRICKHOWELL CASTLE

Wales has more castles per square mile than any other country in Europe. A fine example of that statistic can be found on the southern border of Powys where the castles at Crickhowell and Tretower are located. Just 3 miles apart, the castles may look somewhat similar, but that's where it ends, as both have very different tales to tell.

Just over the border of Monmouthshire and into Powys, some five miles from the larger market town of Abergavenny, lies Crickhowell. With the A40 road running through its town centre, this charming little town commands stunning views along the Usk valley, with its castle ruins just off the main thoroughfare with easy access.

Crickhowell Castle is one of the major castles of medieval Brycheiniog and was originally a timber stronghold of a motte and bailey, probably built by the Turberville family in the 12th century.

In 1272, the castle was rebuilt in stone with a circular shell stone keep, said by some to resemble the surviving stone keep at Cardiff Castle today. The rebuilding was in line with the basic plan which was conceived by Sir Grimbald Paunceforte, who had a Turberville heiress.

During the 14th century Crickhowell Castle, or Alisby's Castle as it's also known, was in Mortimer hands before being restored to Sir John Paunceforte, great grandson of Sir Grimbald, who by royal command refortified the castle.

At its strongest, the castle would of consisted of a shell keep on a motte, a shell gatehouse, and stone wall, with towers, circling the outer ward. The gatehouse and towers being the last additions to this now ivy covered ruin.

The forces of Owain ap Gruffudd, otherwise known as Owain Glyndwr, left the castle in ruins, before it was eventually granted to Sir William Herbert some years later.

By the mid 16th century the castle was abandoned.

The castle is situated in the town itself, just off the town centre in a park. It is situated 12 miles south-east of Brecon on the A40, alternatively, follow the A40 out of Abergavenny to the north-south-east of Brecon on the A40, alternatively, follow the A40 out of Abergavenny to the north-west.

Situated 3 miles north-west of Crickhowell off the A479 lies Tretower, the name being derived from its resident tower and glorious late-medieval house, which reside there.

The castle was founded by the Norman knight Picard at the turn of the 11th century, and consisted of an earth and timber construction.

This stronghold raised by Picard was a motte which, and very unusually, had the feature of being revetted in stone as it was built. This would normally be a further defensive step added at a later date but it appears that the revettment continued on above the motte to form a polygonal shell.

The motte had a base diameter of between 80 and 90 feet and was surrounded by a ditch some 30 feet wide.

Tretower Castle was to fall into the hands of the Welsh twice, in 1233 and in 1322, but it is between these two uprisings in this period of history, that the castle saw its major structural improvements and more than likely after the first time capture, that the bailey was added.

The wooden buildings on the motte were replaced in stone, probably by Roger Picard or possibly his son John. A tall round keep was erected in the middle of the polygonal shell on the motte.

The tower was built to three storeys with nine feet thick walls. It's entrance was to be on the first floor level, leading into residential rooms with windows set in deep embrasures. All rooms having large fireplaces for its occupants. Today, a slight offset is noticeable in the tower, and this marks the level of the building of the third stage which took place slightly later than the previous two stages.

This round keep is typical of castles constructed in the 13th century and from a military perspective, provided the resident garrison with a perfect 360° field of fire on any attacking force. At its time, this was considered at the forefront of military thinking.

Tretower Castle was listed in 1403 as a defensible stronghold for the current King Henry IV. In 1404, the forces of Owain Glyndwr arrived to take the castle for the Welsh, but with Sir James Berkeley in charge of the defending garrison, the castle withstood the siege and with it, justification that Tretower did indeed merit its 'stronghold' title.

Living conditions within the tower of the castle were now becoming cramped, and the occupants looked to move out into better accommodation which was being built close by, in the form of Tretower Court as we know it today.

As more peaceful times came to Tretower, the castle passed into the hands of Sir Roger Vaughan who in the 15th century, developed Tretower Court into much of how we see at present.

The court forms as much a part of the set-up at Tretower as its castle, in so much as where the castle history tends to tail off, the history then picks up as attention shifted away from it and into the court, which became the focal point of the generations to come.

The construction appears to have taken on four phases, as generation after generation have altered it to their own tastes. The north range dating the earliest, from the 14th century, with the west range dating from the 15th century. With additions in the late 15th century being the third phase and all three being modified again, Charles Vaughan would have carried out the fourth phase in the early part of the 17th century, with the current courtyard reflecting his ideals.

It is interesting to note, that the addition of the wall-walks added in phase three around the 1480's, resulted in a plan similar to the colleges at Oxford and Cambridge.

Generations of the Vaughan family continued to live here, with the notable poet Henry Vaughan, 'the Silurist', residing at the court.

The last major alterations were carried out in the 1630's when classical-style windows of that era were inserted around the courtyard.

Other buildings surrounding the court have since been converted into more practical needs of the times, barns and sheds, and with a further few alterations carried out, it has had its original medieval look disguised. It does however not detract from the fact that it is still one of finest examples of a fortified manor in Wales.

Whereas Crickhowell Castle is available for public visiting throughout the year, Tretower is open daily to the public from March until late October.

Head out of Crickhowell heading north-west along the A479. Situated in the village of Tretower itself, some 3 miles away. In total, 9 miles north-west of Abergavenny. For further information telephone (01874) 730279.

USK CASTLE, CAERLEON CASTLE AND NEWPORT CASTLE

With the towns of Usk and Caerleon, together with larger Newport within easy driving distance of each other, visiting three castles in the same locality will give any amateur historian a great insight into the rich, colourful and varied past of this trio of southern Welsh fortresses.

As Usk Castle is our starting point, an appointment to view the castle will need to be booked prior to any visit, as it's in private ownership. The contact number is at the end of the article.

Usk lies 6 miles east of Pontypool off the

A499, and is a charming rural location, with a river of the same name running nearby, just off the town's centre.

Apart from the Gwent Rural Life Museum which boasts thousands of exhibits, Usk has a Norman castle, the remains of which have been partially converted into a private house.

The ruins as we see them today, reflect well the proportions of the original, although all told, they date back to at least four phases of different building work carried out there.

The castle and town are thought to have been founded in 1120. The earliest part of the castle is the earthen work of the inner ward, which contains a small square keep.

The castle was founded by Richard Strongbow de Clare, and declared a Marcher Lord Stronghold.

The Welsh captured the castle in 1174 despite de Clare's strengthening building work, which is thought to have included the erection of the tower keep. The castle was recaptured in 1184.

William Marshall, earl of Pembroke is credited with replacing the bailey palisade with a masonry wall and round towers, but despite the 'upgrade', the castle was again captured in 1233 during the war of the same year between Richard Marshal and Henry III. It was later recaptured.

The impressive north east round tower is said to have been added by Gilbert IV de Clare in the 1260's, around the same decade as the castle being captured another time, once gain, only to be recaptured later.

When Gilbert V de Clare was killed at the Battle of Bannockburn in 1314, Usk Castle came into the ownership of Elizabeth de Burgh who carried out the further building work, with the erection of the hall block and a chapel. After de Burgh's time, the castle passed to the Mortimers, who walled in the outer bailey on the south, with one round tower and a gatehouse.

During the conquests of Owain Glyndwr, the town was burnt in 1402 and again in 1405, but during my research, I found no substantial evidence to suggest that the castle surrendered to him at this time.

Usk Castle then became part of the Duchy of Lancaster and whilst the castle slipped into decay, the outer gatehouse faired better, being incorporated into a house built in the 1680's to accommodate Thomas Herbert.

Today, Usk Castle is reached by lane along Raglan Road, standing on a hill on the northernmost point of Usk.

Usk's neighbouring castle at Caerleon, is situated 3 miles north-east of Newport off the A449.

Perhaps better known for its overwhelming Roman influence, Caerleon Castle is in its own right, a Norman castle. The invaders used this site for the steep motte of their castle in 1085.

The motte has a tower, a two-towered barbican at the bottom and the strong bailey eventually had two towers of which one survives today, this probably built in the middle of the 13th century.

Like Usk, the castle was attacked but records show it fell just once into Welsh hands, in 1217, with another later attack in 1231 being repelled.

Caerleon Castle may not be a grandiose spectacle, but it is never the less, an important part of history and should not be overlooked in favour of just Roman architecture.

From Caerleon Castle to Newport Castle, situated at the east end of Newport High Street, and sadly squeezed and contorted to meet modern building and road demands, surely not how a castle should be treated?. Never the less, it still stands, a testimony to both CADW and the Norman invaders architecture.

The Normans founded the castle in 1172, and since its later rebuilding in following centuries, the original form it took is unclear.

Situated on the banks of the River Usk, Newport Castle replaces an earlier stronghold of a motte and bailey castle, at the top of Stow Hill, near the cathedral.

The castle at its new site was built between 1327 and 1386 by Hugh d'Audele or possibly his son-in-law, Ralph, earl of Stafford.

At the time, Newport was the headquarters of the Norman lordship of Wentloog, and the new castle reflected Wentloog's status as a separate lordship in its own right, having been in the lordship of Glamorgan until 1314.

It wasn't until the second part of the 15th century that any further building work was to take place. To accompany the typically medieval look to the castle, (a curtain wall enclosing a courtyard, a gatehouse and towers), it was strengthened and embellished along grand lines by Humphrey Stafford, later the first duke of Buckingham.

The most important alterations were the raising of the north curtain wall and the heightening and modernising of the south tower from two to three storeys.

Like Usk and Caerleon, Newport Castle weathered its fair share of attacks and captures during the 13th century, again in 1321, and once more by Owain Glyndwr in 1404.

Following the beheading of the 3rd duke of Buckingham, the castle fell into disrepair and by the 18th century was mostly ruins. Restoration work is attributed to its state today.

In the middle of the Newport Castle is the central tower and when looking from the west, it is possible to make out all of the principal features, including the water-gate beneath.

To the south of the central tower was a long narrow room and in the tower here, the lord's apartments would have been and judging by the quality of the decorated windows, fireplaces and carved corbels on the upper floor, sophistication and comfort was the order of the day.

For appointments to view Usk Castle, telephone *(01291) 672563*. Both Caerleon Castle and Newport Castle can be seen all year around.

W

WHITE CASTLE

If you venture out Skenfrith way towards Llantilio Crosenny in Monmouthshire, along the B4521 until you sight the CADW signs, your journey eventually brings you to the site of the White Castle, a well preserved piece of history waiting to be rediscovered.

White Castle, so-called because during its many changes of ownership it was covered in a gleaming light plaster, makes up the 'Three Castles', purposely built as a triangle of fortresses to guard the threat of the Welsh from Gwent. The other castles being at Skenfrith and Grosmont respectively. Together the castles controlled the routes from England into Wales, defending the open countryside that lay between the cliffs of the Wye Valley and the Black Mountains to the north-west. In particular, Skenfrith was built to guard crossings over the river Monnow.

There seems to be some conflict over what might have been on this site before any major construction of a castle took place in the late 12th century, from a small timber fort to an earthwork stronghold. Whichever is correct, there was certainly some form of defensive post earlier on. Work that has been chronicled before the main building commenced,

dates from between 1138 and 1155. In 1161, on the royal accounts of Henry II, there is mention of charges being made for repairs at Llantilion, Skenfrith and Grosmont castles. We must presume that Llantillio Castle as it was then known, is indeed White Castle as it stands today.

In 1201, White, or Llantilio at the time, Grosmont and Skenfrith were granted by King John to Hubert de Burgh, and by 1205, had come into the possession of William de Braose who along with his men in 1176, had carried out the brutal murders of a group of Welsh chiefs at nearby Abergavenny Castle, during a so-called 'peace conference'.

William de Braose then fell from favour with King John only to have his son recover it for the family at the end of the King's reign. With the death of John in 1216, Henry III would succeed him and by 1219, Hubert de Burgh, by now Justiciar and Earl of Kent, was awarded back the 'Three Castles' by the King's Court.

Hubert de Burgh was himself then to fall from favour in 1232 and the nephew of the Bishop of Winchester, Peter des Rivaux was given the 'Three Castles' custody.

During 1233, Henry III was to visit the other castle of the 'three', Grosmont, (big hill), with his Queen. The castle was to be captured by Richard de Clare during his stay and he, his wife and other castle occupants were forced to flee into the darkness of a night attack.

In 1234, Peter des Rivaux's career came to an end and the 'Three Castles' were to become property of the Crown, under the direction of German Waleran. It was under his charge, that most of the work on the castle was done in 1244.

It is also at this time that White Castle would have taken its name, from the plaster placed upon its walls, some of which can still be seen today.

Next to have ownership of the castle was Prince Edward, who later went on to become Edward I. Edward invested much money in strengthening the defences at White Castle, solely due to the increased threat by the Welsh, under Llewelyn, Prince of Wales.

Llewelyn and Edward were bitter rivals. Edward had watched powerless from the walls of Chester Castle, as Llewelyn occupied his 'Four Cantref', (part of Gwynedd). Such frustration was to be well remembered when Edward succeeded the throne in 1272.

As for White Castle, the change of hands continued when Edward in turn was to give the castle to his younger brother, the Earl of Lancaster.

On 10th November 1277, following many battles, Llewelyn made peace with Edward at the signing of the Treaty of Rhuddlan. Llewelyn was to pay him huge sums of money in tribute to him, but did retain the title of Prince of Wales. In fact, for a time their 'understanding' flourished, with Edward even giving Eleanor de Montford, (daughter of Simon de Montford, leader of the English barons), away at her wedding to Llewelyn, and he even paid the bill for their reception!.

The bitter rivalry between the two was to soon resurface, with Edward vowing to crush the Welsh under Llewelyn once and for all.

It wasn't until 1282 that this was to come to an end, with Llewelyn's death, whose head was taken to Tower Bridge to be displayed as a traitor.

Some doubt surrounds Llewelyn's death, and why he was separated from the rest of his forces whilst defending a bridge near Builth Castle. Llewelyn, seen riding on his own, was run through by the lance of Adam de Frankton, who didn't even know it was Llewelyn.

White Castle, which had made up the front line of defence should Abergavenny Castle fall, was destroyed along with many other fortresses, and its usefulness as a military stronghold, was gone forever.

Many years past until the Castle was sold to the Duke of Beaufort in 1825, and then in 1922, the Government was appointed its custody by its owner, Sir Henry Mather Jackson. Skenfrith Castle, was given to the National Trust in 1936, and its guardianship entrusted to the Department of the Environment.

Today, White Castle is one of the best surviving examples of a ring castle. It has a large outer ward, enclosed by its own walls and towers, then a self contained inner ward encircled by a substantial moat. In the 13th Century, most of the keep was demolished, and replaced by six impressive round towers, four of them at intervals around the curtain, and the other two forming the towers of the gateway, approached via the then drawbridge and now permanent wooden bridge, across the deeply-sunken water filled moat.

White Castle appears to have always been used solely for military purposes, despite there have being a chapel, hall and kitchen in the inner ward. It is more likely to have been the residence of a garrison commander, than any nobleman.

The gatehouse can still be accessed to give superb views all around of the countryside and Skirrid mountain.

During the summer months, the Castle is open between 10 a.m. and 5 p.m. and an 'Open Site' during the winter.

Situated at Llantilio Crosenny, 6 miles east-north-east of Abergavenny, between the B4233 and the B4521. Limited but free parking. For further information telephone (01600) 780380.

ABOUT THE AUTHOR

Jonathan is a freelance broadcaster/writer, working out of Abergavenny in Monmouthshire, South Wales. His freelance work is carried out alongside a daytime job as an auditor for an international company. Also during weekdays, he broadcasts the weather on GTFM 106.9, with several daytime slots reaching 200,000 listeners.

Jonathan was part of the BAFTA award winning writing team for the third series of 'The Fast Show,' which was screened on BBC Two, and sold globally to over 30 countries.

Other work includes, being part of a writing team for the regional comedy sketch show, 'The Comedy Show,' screened on HTV Wales, and work on a pilot show for BBC TV entitled 'Yes Sir I Can Boogie,' which was produced by Ash Atalla, the man who has produced many shows for the BBC, including the BAFTA award winning 'The Office.'

Jonathan has also broadcast on BBC Radio 4; BBC Radio Wales; BBC Radio Gwent; Valleys Radio; BRFM and NHSound, covering a wide range of topics, both as a presenter and an interviewee.

Topics include the weather; castles; astronomy; television programme reviews and previews, and current affairs. He also picked up a credit on the long running BBC Radio Two show 'The News Huddlines', for his comedy input.

Apart from castles, his other interests include meteorology, with 22 weekly newspaper columns on the weather, stretching from Hereford down to Carmarthen. Also astronomy, having written several freelance articles for the national magazine Astronomy Now, and having had a regular column in the Abergavenny Chronicle which ran for 7 years, later moving on to write for the Monmouthshire Beacon.

Jonathan also has a weekly TV Preview column in the South Wales Argus produced newspaper, the Free Press.

Other work has included a stint in the BBC Wales newsroom, compiling news for Wales Today; BBC Radio Wales; BBC Radio Cymru and S4C.

His castle passion includes a three year affair with Country Quest magazine, with articles on castles being published monthly, and a series of 5 articles in the Free Press during the Summer of 2004, plus discussing the topic on radio and becoming involved with the local history society in Abergavenny.

Jonathan is also involved with voluntary work for Nevill Hall Sound hospital radio in Abergavenny, pioneering the only live news output for the area, that is produced and broadcast from within the area.

Why not visit Jonathan's website?

www.theworldofjonathanpowell.org.uk

Printed in the United States
By Bookmasters